SAVIOR

Stefanie Dawn

Savior
Elements of Abduction
Book 1

Stefanie Dawn

Disclaimer: The material in this book contains graphic language and sexual content and is intended for mature audiences, ages 18 and older.

ISBN: 978-1763870482

Editing and Proofing by Swish Design & Editing
Book Design by Swish Design & Editing
Cover Design by Eric at
The Book Brander
Published by Angels and Fire Books
Cover Image Copyright 2023

DEDICATION

For everyone who came here for
giant alien cock...
You won't be disappointed.

SAVIOR

CHAPTER

I

ILK

Ten Earth Years Ago

Two full cycles of the planet around the sun since my brother, Lanir, and I had seen each other. Two cycles of the sun, each containing two seasons per cycle, our planet was perfect for the creation and sustaining of life. Unfortunately, it was also home to the Ghaal, a cruel species who used to dominate the planet but now withered on the edges of extinction.

Lanir and I found ourselves together again after so long apart because we were drawn away from our solitary homes by the same thing.

The scent of death.

Of the six of us, Lanir and I were the only ones who lived close enough to the colony to have picked up on the scent, and it was no surprise to either of us the stench of blood was coming from near where the Ghaals called home. But the scent wasn't Ghaal blood nor the blood of any animal I knew, and equal parts rage and horror burned inside me when I realized what it meant.

The Ghaal had found more species to experiment on.

As I moved across the base of the mountains, I couldn't decide if being the closest to the Ghaal colony, and therefore the one who needed to investigate, was a blessing or a curse. I could control myself better than Lanir, who had suffered more than most of us at the hands of the Ghaal and eventually became the animal they treated him as.

Perhaps it *was* best I was here. I may be the only one who had hope of controlling Lanir when his rage undoubtedly took hold.

Coming around behind Lanir as he crouched low between the boulders, I grabbed his arm. He'd arrived before me, moving with stealth through the base of the mountains from the opposite direction I had. The boulders near his home were comprised of the volcanic rock from the harmless volcano on which we both now stood. We were camouflaged well, his skin almost the same color as the rocks, and although mine was lighter from my home on the other side of the mountain, I too, was able to find a spot to blend in.

Lanir snarled at me and tried to dislodge my hand from his arm with a shake, an animalistic reaction to my unwanted physical contact. I held him still and watched his reaction cautiously. It seemed solitary life had only increased his aggression, and while not ideal, there wasn't much I could do about it. It was important we remained separated from each other, from all our brothers. There was work to do, a need greater than our individual desires for company.

The singular Ghaal came into view, carrying a body over his shoulder, and Lanir's muscles tensed under my touch, ready to pounce. I gripped him harder, and a growl rumbled through his chest. We wanted information, and for that, we needed to watch the Ghaal, for now at least. Lanir had suffered greatly. Even now, I remember the pain in his eyes as he was forced into a transformation he couldn't help.

Shaking the thought from my head, I was lurched back to the present moment when, with a snarl, Lanir launched himself over the boulder in front of him, the stone crumbling slightly under his weight as he used it to vault, and his hands landing heavily on a Ghaal's shoulders. A quick glance confirmed the Ghaal was alone, and he fell heavily under Lanir's bulk. We were taller and stronger than the

Ghaal, designed to be the best DNA could offer. I scowled as Lanir held the Ghaal still, annoyed I hadn't prevented or delayed his attack.

Left with no choice, I moved out from my hiding space and stopped at the sight in front of me.

The scent of blood was overwhelming as the wind picked up, slamming the odor into my face and making my stomach lurch. Though the blood splashed across the ground in front of me and down the front of the Ghaal's uniform was red, not greenish-gray, the coppery scent was unmistakable.

A female, a species I didn't recognize, her torso had been haphazardly sewn back together after being cut open and no doubt experimented on. Her skin was pale and her eyes milky as they stared unseeingly at the sky. Her golden hair flowed from her head in knotted waves, now caked with blood. She had no fur or hair on her arms or legs but a small tuft of dark hair between her legs.

She was not Ghaal, nor was she Synth like me. I'd never seen this species before, but she looked small and in need of protection. My brothers and I had been unable to protect her, and my stomach churned at the thought. We tried to save everyone, all species, from the hands of the Ghaal. But sometimes it wasn't possible, and the evidence of my failure was dead on the rocks in front of me.

The Ghaal acquired species to experiment on in

an attempt to use them for breeding by nefarious means, and it was part of the reason my brothers and I separated from each other. The abducted species—always delivered by units that were dropped to the surface by transporters—were our duty. If we could get to them first and steer them from the Ghaal, they would be safe.

The units stopped abruptly for a while, and a red dome flashed across the sky—a signal to ships the Galactic Empire had discovered what the Ghaal were doing with the abductees, and they were cut off from trade and interaction with other planets.

We were stuck here now.

We all were.

I struggled to contain my rage at the thoughts of what this female would have suffered at the hands of the Ghaal. How long had they had her? I tried to pull the timeline together. She must have been acquired before the Ghaal were cut off from transporters.

A full month, maybe a few weeks?

Minutes would be too long to be in their hands.

Lanir growled through his own similar musings as I watched the Ghaal squirming in Lanir's grip.

"What did you do to her?" I barely managed to keep my voice even as I kneeled next to the Ghaal male before me, still pinned under Lanir. His orange eyes glowed as he glared at me, and I blinked back at him, waiting for the information I'd requested.

Lanir didn't wait and snapped his teeth at the Ghaal, who dragged his gaze to the being on top of him, the first flicker of concern I'd seen passing across his expression. "Why are you so violent? That's not how we created you. You should be submissive," he said, his voice void of emotion.

The Ghaal recoiled as Lanir snapped at him again, narrowly missing his throat with his sharp teeth, and I found my urge to avoid violence waning as the scent of the female's blood continued to invade my nostrils, the Ghaal unconcerned with the damage he had created.

"I'm what you made me," Lanir snarled at him, and the Ghaal's eyes widened slightly before he rolled his head to look at me, almost a plea in his eyes that I protect him from my brother. A plea he would rather die than voice out loud.

"They'll notice if I don't return," he said.

"What did you do to her?" I repeated. I knew he was right. If he didn't return to the colony, others might come in search of him. But my brother and I were stronger than ten of them, and with their population dwindling, they wouldn't risk that many lives to save one who had wandered into our territory. I suspect this Ghaal knew that.

A snarl I couldn't help grated through my throat when the Ghaal *smiled* at me. His hard beak-like lips pulled back to reveal his sharp teeth and black tongue. "We have found our answer, and we no longer need you."

"You killed her," I snarled out, curling my hands into fists.

"We'll get more of them, the human females. They are the answer we've been seeking, and we'll simply get *more*. The sacrifice of this lot was a small price to pay. We had to be absolutely sure they were right. They didn't make it, but it was worth it."

Lanir and I exchanged glances before looking again at the female's body. If the Ghaal had suspected the species was compatible with them for breeding purposes, they would have cut them up and experimented endlessly to make absolutely sure. Perhaps they had even successfully impregnated one or more of them, but with their failing technology, surgical proof was the next best thing. When the Ghaal experimented, they did so in sixes—always in sixes—because even the most intelligent and advanced beings had superstitions.

They wouldn't do anything if they didn't have six.

If what the Ghaal said was true, all six females taken were killed in the process, suffering greatly before they finally died at the hands of a cruel and indifferent species.

"But you've lost the treaty," Lanir spoke the words I had been thinking before I could. We'd both seen the red veil shimmer in the atmosphere when the last transport ship had departed all those weeks ago, indicating this planet was now off-limits for intergalactic trade. "They found out what you were doing and won't help you now. You can't get more."

I ground my teeth together. The knowledge the Ghaal had lost intergalactic trade because of the innocents they had killed crawled under my skin. The other species we hadn't been able to get to in time would have suffered the same fate.

Again, the Ghaal smiled, and I seethed with hatred for the species before me. They had no regard for others. Their own fates were their only concern—*save the remaining Ghaal and increase the population at* any *cost.* But there were so few of them now, existing in an ever-dwindling colony with old and obsolete technology they no longer had the expertise to maintain. All the technology specialists were dead or had left the planet with the final evacuation a generation ago.

Even if they *had* found a compatible species, surely no transporters would help them kidnap innocent females if they knew their fate.

"There are always those who are willing to do dirty work for a price." He sneered at me, and his smile fell from his hard lips seconds before Lanir's fist came down, cracking the Ghaal's skull with the force of the blow as he connected with his forehead. The Ghaal stared at me with his one remaining open eye, communicating a world of thoughts through that look. He knew I wouldn't save him, and perhaps I *couldn't* against Lanir's rage. Despite my hatred for violence, maybe part of me didn't want to act. My brothers and I promised we wouldn't resort to violence.

All of us but Lanir.

He was untamable.

Lanir hit the Ghaal repeatedly until his head was nothing more than a sticky pulp on the rocks. I looked away, staring out over the tree line between us and the ocean shore where the Ghaal colony resided. Should we simply have gone in there and killed them all? We thought once we left the Ghaal—since their technology was mostly in disrepair and they were still fighting and killing amongst themselves—they wouldn't last long.

They proved us wrong.

And perhaps my stance on no violence wouldn't hold.

But it might not be as simple as that.

The Ghaal created the Synth, and if they managed to capture us, they could end us. We escaped out of sheer desperation and violence, not an act I hoped to repeat.

Lanir stood, and I scolded him, "Violence is not the answer, Lanir."

He glared at me. "Violence is the *only* thing they understand."

The Ghaal had said they'd found their answer, which meant the female of the species who now lay dead at our feet was a match for breeding or close enough they could make it work.

They'd need more fertile females, and if they'd found them...

I tried not to let my thoughts stray too far down that path. Lanir was correct. Killing an innocent species would have been the thing that broke the treaty they had with the intergalactic transport missions. But the Ghaal was also correct in that there were species who were quite capable and willing to kidnap whoever and whatever they liked if the price was right. Our planet may no longer have riches and coin, but we have an abundance of natural fuel and resources. The Ghaal would find a way to exploit this to get more of the female species they required.

My thoughts brought me back to the present, and I glanced sadly at the female body. She deserved a proper burial, and Lanir and I exchanged a glance before I picked up the body. We wouldn't drop her into one of the lava pits for quick disposal as the Ghaal had no doubt been intending. Instead, we would find a place to give her a respectful burial.

I wished I knew her name.

Maybe we should give her one.

Watching Lanir walk ahead of me, it struck me how different we had become. Having adapted to slightly different environments, physically, we no longer looked like brothers, except for our eyes.

Two years ago, we and our other four brothers

had escaped the Ghaal colony, refusing to help them rebuild their dying species. We were created for breeding as synthetic organisms, intelligent and alive, but ultimately developed in a lab—a dying scientist's last gift to his dwindling species. The best of their lab-created DNA, we were able to adapt to our environments, and that included changing our gender.

But we didn't want to help the Ghaal, steadfastly remaining male until it almost broke us, and we eventually escaped them.

Now they were getting desperate.

From my new home—a cave around the other side of the mountains—I'd seen the transport ships landing, and for a short while, I'd foolishly assumed they were swapping technology in exchange for supplies from our planet. But it seemed they were trading something far more sinister even before using units to drop the *goods*—innocent species to be used for experimentation until a suitable breeding match could be found.

The units started being dropped when the ship wouldn't land after my brothers and I attacked one. We decided to separate from each other to cover as much ground as possible and steer what species we could away from harm. We loved each other, but living together was proving difficult, and as hard as it was being alone, it was the best way.

The units landed haphazardly.

If we could get to them before the Ghaal, we could save them.

But the intergalactic transporters knew what the Ghaal was doing now. I had no idea what the Ghaal *told* them they were doing with the kidnapped species and why they thought it was okay. But different classes of planets, not part of the galactic union, may not have the same lawful protection as others. Maybe they assumed the species were nothing more than animals and deserved no respect, or perhaps they thought they would be used as pets or servants. But from the introduced species I had met, I knew that wasn't often the case. They were intelligent and afraid of the fate that had been shoved upon them.

The last time the transporters departed, a flash of red accompanied them when they left the atmosphere. A warning remained to other vessels—this planet was now a no-trade zone.

But the Ghaal was correct—there were always pirates. Since the remaining Ghaal could no longer leave the planet, they must rely on others willing to do their dirty work.

The Ghaal must have been desperate to kill the female if she were indeed compatible with them.

Desperate and *certain* they could get more.

When Lanir and I reached the edge of the rocky outcrop of the mountains, Lanir kept walking. I followed him in silence as he made his way along the edge of the cliff line until he stopped at a spot that looked out over the ocean.

"We'll bury her here," he said without inflection and got to work digging the grave with his bare hands. Locating some water, I ripped a section from my loincloth to use as a rag and wiped as much of the blood from the female's face and body as I could. Would she normally wear clothes? I didn't know. Were there any burial rites her species would partake in? Religions? Superstitions? I knew nothing of her. Somewhere galaxies away, she might have a family wondering what became of her. The thought forced a growl through my chest, the sound echoing from Lanir even though my brother kept his eyes downcast and continued to dig.

She was dead—Lanir and I knew this. But we had enough respect for the innocent female to give her a proper burial as we could manage.

"We should give her a name," I said as I kneeled next to the fresh mound of soil he had dug up.

Lanir studied her face, a softness coming across his features before his brows drew together again, and his expression hardened. "*Laloisa.*"

It was perfect.

A word I hadn't heard in many decades, roughly translating to the feeling one gets when watching the sunset.

Gently, I lowered Laloisa into the hand-dug grave and again wished I knew her real name or anything about her that we could say. But there were no words to say except, "Goodbye, Laloisa, I wished better for you." We filled in the dirt, stood and brushed ourselves off, and stared out at the ocean.

"They'll find a way to get more of these females," I said, and Lanir simply grunted but didn't turn to look at me. "And when they do, we must be ready to save them from this fate. No matter how long we have to wait or how long it takes, they'll get more."

"I know," he grunted out.

Staying apart from my brothers indefinitely wouldn't be easy, but to save more innocents from the hands of the Ghaal, we would do what needed to be done.

CHAPTER 2

ERICA

Present Day

There are many things movies and television shows don't cover about alien abduction.

First, and most important of all, is that it is *real*. In fact, up until the moment I was taken, I would've *argued* that aliens didn't exist, and if they did exist, they sure as hell didn't come to Earth.

What a fun way to be proven wrong.

Second is how absolutely bone-achingly cold it is on a spaceship. I'm still trying to figure out how they have the technology to travel through space, but they can't turn the heating up to a more comfortable temperature. Maybe this is why they didn't come to the surface. Perhaps it was too hot for them, opting instead to use their technology to grab us from our beds.

Or maybe they were simply lazy.

Why come down to the surface of a foreign planet when you can press a button and have a beam of light do it for you?

All of it was speculation because they were *aliens,* and I didn't understand anything about what was going on.

No amount of scrambling to hold on to my mattress and bedsheets was enough to keep me grounded, and I prayed for gravity to suddenly increase in strength tenfold to make their beams really work for it. Even if I couldn't escape, I wanted them to have to fight for it, and I punched and kicked at the air the entire way up. Apparently, the idea that if the beam did lose hold of me, I would plummet to the ground was something that, in the moment, didn't occur to me. But instead of them having to work for it, I was slipped from my house through the newly created hole in my roof—*there goes my deposit*—and sent tumbling upside down into the icy depths of their ship. Struggling to keep my panic at bay and the contents of my stomach where they should be, I crossed the threshold from the chill of the night into the aching cold of the inside of a sterile aircraft without my fighting having any effect.

What they *do* tell you in the movies and what they got right is that there are probes.

Though, thankfully, nothing had been inserted up my butt. Yet.

The second I was deposited on the cold floor, the aliens approached me with curvy, white instruments that so closely resembled those pelvic exam ultrasound wands, I clamped my legs together on instinct. I tried running but made it about six steps before I ran directly into a group of them and was unceremoniously slammed onto my back. The instruments were jammed into my ears, mouth, and belly button, pushing so hard I cried out. I could only hope they got whatever readings they needed from those intrusions alone.

Unable to get the assault from my mind, I gently touched my stomach, now tender and bruised from their rough handling.

I was screamed out. I simply had nothing left to give from my lungs and throat, dried and painful. I'd screamed and sobbed and fought. I'd tried to run several times and kicked out at them whenever they got near, but none of it made any difference. Perhaps I'd be less bruised if I had given up and become a limp ragdoll for them to do with what they will. But then again, maybe if I didn't holler and kick and carry on, they would have kept going with their probes, and something worse would have happened than a bruised belly button and sore ears. My instinct was to fight with every ounce of strength I had, which wasn't much, admittedly, but I would fight every step of the way, no matter what. Once they were done probing, I was dragged, still kicking, before being pushed into a cage. I'd screamed for hours, initially screaming for help and then reduced to screaming a long, loud tone of pure terror that echoed off the walls around me and assaulted my eardrums until I couldn't take the sound anymore.

They'd ushered me into a clear, hard cube, suspended a few feet from the floor of the ship, and while I still had the strength, I screamed at the aliens every time they passed the outside of the cube, but if they could hear me, they ignored the noise. I could be thankful that, at least inside the cube, it wasn't as cold as it was in the rest of the ship. The floor may have been uncomfortable, but it hummed quietly, just enough I could hear if I pressed my ear to the flat surface, and it was warm enough to spread my fingers out along it and let it soothe my aches.

The suits the aliens wore covered their features and bodies from my sight, and I wasn't sure if this was a mercy or not. Would it be better to know what I was faced with? They were small and roundish, the lower part of their body rotund and balancing on two small legs with big flat feet that slapped on the floor as they waddled with surprising speed. Their arms were long and thin and held no weapons, but ended in large, flat hands, almost as big as their feet but with only two fingers and a thumb twice the length and width of the fingers. They appeared lopsided, their proportions completely out of whack, and I wondered how they moved about. But maybe I looked as strange to them as they did to me.

The difference was, of course, they were not frightened of *me*, and *I* was the one in the cage.

Their helmets had a single panel in the front which I assumed they saw through, but I couldn't begin to guess how many eyes they had or how big they were, or if they even *had* eyes.

And I had enough whirling around in my mind without concentrating too hard on what I couldn't see.

My suspicions grew that my cube was soundproof.

The aliens seemed much too good at ignoring me for the sound to be getting through. Curled up in the corner of my cube, I stood at attention when another girl was brought into the room, the white doors sliding shut behind her as she kicked and fought with the aliens pulling her toward her cube. Rushing to the side, I pressed my palms against the cube, slapping the wall and screaming, hoping she could hear me.

Her eyes shifted to mine, and her glossy black hair fell in front of her face. While her eyes widened when she saw me trapped, instead of fear, there was rage flaring behind her eyes, and she started fighting anew. I cheered her on as three more aliens came to help restrain her, and while she wouldn't be much taller than me, she was obviously fitter, and they struggled to keep her under control. She landed a punch to one alien's face, and I cheered her on as she ran toward the control panel, slamming her fists into it and causing an uproar from the aliens. I smacked my palms on the cube wall, screaming for her to look out, but she didn't hear me, and she was knocked out when one of the aliens brought down one of their white instruments across her head.

Unconscious, she was dragged into the cube opposite mine, maybe only five feet away, but it might as well have been five miles. After a while, I stopped banging on the cube and sank to my knees, hands still pressed against the wall and watching her, praying she was okay.

When she regained consciousness, I found out for sure the cubes were soundproof.

She raced up and down the small space, and when the aliens ignored her as they did me, fear finally took her over. She screamed, her mouth and features contorted with fear as she beat against the walls before sinking into a ball, her shoulders shaking. I wanted to help her, to at least hold her until she stopped crying. Whoever she was, she was a fighter, and I found myself admiring that part of her. But she was also human, vulnerable, kidnapped, and frightened, and if I couldn't kick ass like she could, I at least wanted to be able to comfort her. But even that luxury, that snippet of humanity, was out of reach here in my cage. It would be nice if, in this hellhole, we could hold each other. Maybe we were being kept separate because the aliens thought we would plot our escape.

They would be right about that, although I don't know what good plotting would do.

After a long while, she raised her head and looked at me, and I lifted my hand in a small, sad wave. She just stared, her eyes again flashing with anger, even though they were rimmed red. I lifted my tank top and pointed to my belly to show her the bruising. She mimicked the gesture, her stomach red, the bruises not yet formed. Frowning, I dropped my tank and watched her. She had been subjected to the same probing, and I shuddered to think what they were looking for.

We just stared at each other, each leaning against the walls of our cubes as close as we could get, which wasn't close at all.

The aliens continued to ignore us, and over the next several hours, other girls were brought in until there were four of us in total. I studied the room through the clear sides of the cubes, each cube tall enough to stand in and maybe take four steps either way, but that was it. They had provided us with no bedding, only the small cube in the corner to relieve ourselves and no toilet paper. The room outside was plastered floor to ceiling with control panels of some sort, but there were no buttons or levers, only smooth black areas with strange text on them. Nothing had happened that I noticed when the black-haired girl slammed her palms onto the control panel. Maybe it was just a screen. However, in places the aliens would touch them, the text would change, but it meant zero to me.

Nothing happened for several hours after the fourth girl was brought in, and I kept waiting for there to be more. We were in separate cubes and watched each other, standing or sitting as close as we could on the edges nearest to the cages closest to our own. It may have been futile, but it was all I could think to do, and apparently, it was an instinct they shared—seeking closeness and comfort we couldn't have.

I didn't wear a watch, and my phone was on my bedside table charging, so I could only guess how much time had passed without an event.

Eight, maybe twelve hours? Initially, I refused to relieve myself in the small white box in the corner of the room, but eventually, I had no choice. I wasn't a prude by any means, but my cheeks still warmed with shame when I awkwardly squatted over the tiny cube, ducking my chin to my chest and refusing to look up until I was done. When I finished, the other girls had averted their eyes, and I was thankful they understood my hesitation. There was no privacy in a clear cube.

I had finished relieving myself when an alien approached the cage, and I was torn between wanting to move toward it or trying to escape and get as far away as possible. I paced, and it waited until I was with my back against the rear wall before it slid in a tray of what I can only assume was food. Its gloved hands slid through the hard side of the cube as though it weren't there.

I didn't eat. The small part of my brain that remained logical told me there would be little sense in them abducting us only to poison us, but that didn't mean the food didn't have some other messed-up side effect. Maybe it would knock me unconscious. After another few hours, I couldn't ignore the rumbling of my stomach any longer, and I tentatively approached the tray and poked at the food—a cube of white gelatinous substance which trembled after I prodded at it.

Still, I didn't eat it, not straightaway.

But being defiant was pointless when our captors didn't seem to give a shit if we ate or not. They weren't watching us or coming into the cube to force-feed us.

Time ticked on, and the other girls and I stared at each other from our cages. The black-haired girl in the cage closest to mine was the first to show bravery, and from the little I knew about her, it seemed apt. She poked again at her white jelly cube, and with her fingers, she broke off a small corner, lifting it to her face and sniffing. Then she licked at it and yanked it away from her face abruptly as if expecting an instant reaction. When nothing happened, she nibbled at it and swallowed. I held my breath, waiting.

She looked up and let her gaze travel between the other girls and me, then with a shrug, she gave an unenthusiastic thumbs up and, with a small grimace, took another bite. The other two girls turned to me as she ate, and I guessed it was my turn now. I followed suit, sniffing and licking it before popping it in my mouth. There was little to no flavor, but I was thankful for the tastelessness, guessing that it was better than it being something so sickly I had to choke it down to avoid starving. When I pressed the jelly-like substance against the roof of my mouth, it released a cool juice that slid down my throat as I chewed, soothing me from all the crying and screaming. I hummed with satisfaction since we had no water, either.

I'd guess it was almost a day after the final girl was abducted and thrown into her cube before a jolt of the ship sent us flying into the sides of our respective cages. After rightening myself, I stayed on all fours, looking around in terror, but none of the aliens seemed concerned, having barely moved with the jolt, their low center of gravity keeping them still. The vibration that had been only a background sensation, had increased in intensity. With another sickening lurch, it whirred to life, jolting only a handful of times before building up to a heavy vibration that made my feet tingle.

I could only guess what it meant, and I didn't like it.

We were moving.

Away from Earth.

Away from home.

And toward God knows what fate.

Were we to be sold? Eaten? Used as slaves or sex toys? Were we fodder for some space alien herd of pigs?

No option seemed good, and somehow, I doubted we'd been abducted to be taken to a faraway planet for a holiday and treated as queens, after which we'd be returned to Earth.

Ridiculous and impossible thoughts.

But they were the ones I held on to as I eventually gave in to exhaustion and slept.

CHAPTER 3

ERICA

The aliens continued to ignore us.

They didn't respond when we pounded on the sides of our cages and screamed at them for answers, and other than delivering food, they barely glanced at us. They never came and emptied our waste containers that we saw, yet somehow every time we went, after they were empty. Small mercies, I guess.

I had no idea how long I would be in this cage and wasn't keen on the idea of it filling up with the smell of my own waste, which I could do nothing about.

Since our initial probing, the aliens seemed completely disinterested in us. *Was that a good or a bad thing?* I couldn't tell. I doubted anything that happened here was a good thing for any of us.

The other women and I had communicated small words by breathing on the glass-like walls of our cages and spelling them out. I had learned their names and simple facts about them because telling each other these things was the closest thing we had to bonding and keeping sane. We also became rather good at charades because spelling could be tiresome.

Tori had just finished mimicking cutting her hair to indicate she was a hairdresser, and looking at her hair, that made sense. It was sensational, and I could picture her in a television ad, flipping it over her shoulder and looking seductively at the camera. *If you use this product, your hair will be flawless too.* Now Misha was doing a small hop step, holding imaginary reins in front of her, her cheek pinched at the corner of her mouth. If I concentrated hard enough, I could hear in my mind the clicking sound she was making to mimic a horse's hooves. When she started spinning an imaginary rope around her head, I almost laughed and looked to see a similar half-smile on Tori's face.

These were my new friends.

Victoria, who preferred to go by Tori, the first girl to come in after me, was a raven-haired beauty with eyes that could kill or seduce, I imagined. She was a twenty-two-year-old hairdresser in the last year of her apprenticeship. I hadn't expected to find out she was a hairdresser after her badass display of fighting the aliens off when she first came in, but I guess I shouldn't judge anything by its cover.

Like my home, for example, I thought that was safe.

Misha, the third girl to come in, with dark hair that sat in tight curls around her face, was a twenty-four-year-old horse trainer who also ran a riding school. She lived alone on a small hobby farm she'd inherited and was worried about her horses and how long it would take someone to find that she was missing and the horses needed rescuing. I tried to assure her they would be fine. She always supplied them plenty of food, but she was still worried.

Samara, a nineteen-year-old teaching assistant with wavy blonde hair that fell down her back, had barely started university. She was petite and looked young and frightened, but maybe my face had an equal expression of terror on it. I couldn't be sure—there were no mirrors.

And me, a twenty-five-year-old who had no idea what to do with her life, currently working as a barista and questioning why she never took survival and self-defense classes. Single and not ready to mingle, unable to maintain any relationships, friendships or otherwise, and now cursing my love of being alone because maybe if I weren't, I wouldn't have been such easy fodder for taking.

The aliens came with food twice a day, still sliding their hand through the hard side of the cube as though it weren't there. By the fourth meal, I had crawled up to the side where they always served from, and although the alien paused before sliding the tray toward me, it no longer waited until I backed away.

A potentially bat-shit crazy plan formed in my mind.

I glanced over to see Tori had been watching me, and after we ate, I stood and moved to the side of my cube. At no point when we'd been communicating had the aliens shown any interest or concern, but even so, I glanced around the room to make sure none of them were looking before I breathed against the glass.

I try escape.

It took a bit of extra concentration to write each time as I had to do the letters and words backward so they were readable from the other side. Occasionally, like now, I did my 'E' the right way around for me out of habit, but she'd be able to figure it out.

Tori's dark eyes studied me. *How?*

Bring food. I escape.

She glanced at her only empty tray on the floor, then back at me. *Then what.*

"Well, shit, Tori, I don't fucking know," I muttered, pausing before writing again. *We all do at same time.*

This time she nodded and pointed at Misha, then between herself and Samara. Right, time to communicate my plan. Misha didn't seem quite as keen as Tori, which is saying something because Tori looked barely convinced. But what else were we going to do? Simply wait until whatever they wanted to do with us happened? Maybe if we could get a weapon, we could force them to take us back home.

The hours until our second meal for the day ticked by slowly, and we spent it pacing our cubes, throwing nervous glances at each other or sitting in the corner and fiddling with what little clothing we were wearing. I felt disgusting after having to use the bathroom bucket without any toilet paper, and I was desperate to get out of here. I had ripped off a strip of fabric from my top, exposing my stomach so I could clean myself. But that rag wouldn't last forever.

Finally, the aliens came to our cubes, carrying the trays, and I shared one last significant look with Tori before dropping to my hands and knees and crawling toward where they usually served our meal. Again, the alien hesitated, but after a moment of staring at me, it shuffled toward the cube.

I waited, and my heart pounded in my ears.

The sound of the tray hitting the floor slammed into my eardrums. It was the loudest and only sound I heard other than my breathing, so I lurched forward and snatched at the alien's hands. It gave a screeching cry of alarm as it pulled on my grip, the sound audible when its hands were passing through the side of the cube. I let it pull, but I moved with it, and waited for my hands to pass through the edge of the cube.

But they didn't.

Where the alien's wrists were penetrating the side of the cube, mine hit the solid edge. I quickly glanced at Tori, who also had the alien's wrists in her grip. However, she was losing it, and after a few seconds, she only clung to its fingers until it was gone. She then slammed her palms against the cube where the alien had disappeared through. The other two girls either missed or had already lost their hold.

I was the last chance.

Looking back at the alien in front of me, still twisting and writhing against my grip, I screamed at it, "Let us go home!" But it ignored me and continued pulling.

I was losing grip. "No, no... *no, no, no!*"

The alien's glove was sliding off, and I scrambled to keep hold of its arms. As its glove slid off, I lurched forward again and snatched at its yellow wrist, wrinkled as though it had been under water for hours.

I screamed.

Yanking my hand away, I let go of the alien, and it retreated out of the cube. My hand felt like it was on fire as if I had snatched a handful of nettles. Its skin was covered in a thin fur that prickled and stuck into mine. Tears sprung to my eyes, and I slid down the cube wall, gripping my wrist as my hand reddened and started to swell before my eyes.

"Ow." I didn't want to be a sook, but the pain was searing and only getting worse. I was crying in earnest when my vision started to gray. *The fucking aliens were poisonous to us?* I didn't even consider that might be an option. I couldn't bring myself to wipe the tears from my face and sobbed loudly as the pain throbbed.

As several of the aliens moved into my cube, I could've sworn I heard a woman's voice calling my name, but maybe that was just wishful thinking.

Slumping to my side, still gripping my wrist, I passed out.

When I woke, the lights in the main room were dimmed as they did every evening when they left for what we could only assume was their night. The lights never went off, only dimmed. I was still in my cube and looked down to find my hand bandaged, the hint of a yellow ointment peeking from beneath the sides of the wrapping. When I flexed my fingers slightly as a test, a shot of pain vibrated up my arm. The pain was nothing compared to when I was originally stung, but it still wasn't pleasant. Without standing, I leaned over toward Tori's cube, and finding her awake, I tapped my wrist where a watch would be if I had one.

She breathed on the glass and wrote out—*three or four hours.*

After a moment, she added—*you okay?*

I lifted a hand and rocked it back and forth—*sort of.*

She nodded and then blew me a kiss before writing—*rest.*

I let myself slump against the wall and tried to sleep.

Every night, at least one of us cried ourselves to sleep, curling up in a ball on the floor since we had no bedding.

Tonight, it was my turn.

The next day, the other girls and I continued our

labored communication, learning that none of us had close families or too many friends.

In other words, no one would miss us much. They would wonder and look, but there wouldn't be a global search. No social media posts or fundraisers for rewards. Just estranged families and friends who were no more than close acquaintances wondering what had become of us.

It was depressing.

This revelation did nothing to soothe any of us, and we sat in silence after the brief conversation, hugging our knees and crying, silent because of the cubes and perhaps the shock. There wasn't much else we could tell about each other. How could we? Stating facts about ourselves gave only a slim idea of the personality of these women, although I still felt bonded to them through our mutual fucked-up situation. Asking questions of each other that none of us had answers for would only increase the stress. I could only assume that, like me, they were swinging wildly between a morose acceptance of our situation and impending deaths and out-of-control, all-consuming panic.

It was difficult to maintain any hope.

The aliens now wouldn't serve us food unless we backed against the opposite side of the cubes, and if we refused, they would point and put their heads through the clear walls of the cubes to screech unpleasantly at us. Further refusal to move away from them would result in no food for that serving. I learned that the hard way.

Eventually, time lost all meaning.

Misha tried several times to make us laugh again with her charades the way she had before, but it didn't work. Any laughter I managed to force out was far from natural. I held her eye contact after she gave up and scrawled on the side of the cube—*thank you for trying*. She blew me a kiss, a gesture that had become our substitute for hugs, and I smiled weakly at her.

It was only a matter of time before they came for us, and we learned our fate.

CHAPTER 4

ERICA

Maybe they not hurt us.

I stared at the words Samara scrawled on the side of her cube, each word printed out one by one after each breath and fading quickly. It had been days. How many, I couldn't be sure. Did the aliens' sense of time even work like hours? Maybe one of our days was two of theirs. It felt like months, but I'm sure it couldn't have been more than one week. Maybe a week and a half?

And nothing had happened.

The aliens still paid no attention to us and simply pushed our twice-daily meals through the walls into our cubes, albeit now with a certain level of trepidation given our escape attempt, and left us to our own devices. They still seemed unconcerned we were communicating with each other. When we first came aboard, we would stop whenever one walked by, tucking our hands behind our backs and pretending we weren't writing on the side of the cubes. But we now did it openly, and it had changed nothing in the aliens' behavior. They didn't care what we did, and all of these things swirled around in my mind as I tried to figure out if it was a good or bad sign we were being ignored.

Samara seemed to have an unwavering sense of hope and positivity, and although she, too, cried herself to sleep on occasion, she always had snippets like this to offer—*maybe they let us go.* Or— *maybe they're friendly.* I wished I had some of that hope. I glanced at Tori's sullen face after reading Samara's latest message, and Tori's thoughts appeared to reflect mine. I can't imagine anything pleasurable coming out of this after being abducted and taken weeks into deep space.

Then again, maybe I didn't want any of Samara's hope because being positive about a situation as fucked up as this could only lead to major disappointment when things inevitably went south.

Maybe—I wrote, pausing—*but what happens after?*

Samara raised her eyes to mine, offering a slight shrug and what could have been a smile if it weren't dashed from her face the moment reality hit her. I hated being her reality check and wiping out whatever sense of hope she was clinging to, but she seemed so naïve, even for her age, and she needed to get with the program along with the rest of us. This wasn't some joy ride. We had been abducted, and there was no version of this where everything was okay.

The vibrating hum of the ship hadn't stopped or even slowed since it started. We'd been whizzing through space to God knows where, and there was nothing we could do about it.

Nothing.

For the past two days, Misha hadn't engaged in the conversations as much as the others did. Instead, she watched it unfold and occasionally nodded if she agreed or pointed to herself as if to say—*me too*—if we were talking about hobbies. But there was no smile and no more attempts to make us laugh. I missed those and wished I had tried harder to show a smile or some amusement so she would know her efforts were appreciated.

I was no pushover, but Tori seemed a force to be reckoned with. Her black hair and brows framed her face. Her features were sharp and kept in an almost permanent frown. She never seemed to stop watching the aliens and what they were doing, and I'd tried that too but resigned myself to the fact I'd never figure out their control panels, even if I did manage to escape the cube. Maybe she was gathering patterns, but if she had learned anything, she hadn't shared it with the rest of us.

Not for the first time, I wished they had caged us together. The smell might be something to contend with, but at least we would have company. Seeing them across a room but unable to touch them, hold their hand, or hug them when they cried was worse than being alone.

But when I woke up screaming or crying, I would look around, and inevitably one of the others would be awake, and we'd shuffle to the sides of our cubes that brought us closest together. We would press our palms against the wall and pretend we could feel their warmth through the icy air outside our cages.

Another day started with the lights brightening to their usual warm glow, but there was no morning meal, and the girls and I exchanged glances when hours went by without one.

This couldn't be good.

One of the aliens came past and stared at me in my cube. It had a small device in its hands—white with a black screen—and looked between me and the device. Feeling bold, I moved across my cube and kneeled in front of the alien, studying the pockmarked suit and its strange flat hands and feet. Whenever it would glance up at me, it was quick, and I couldn't see anything past the viewing panel on its suit. But I already knew what type of skin lay beneath those gloves, and I shuddered, rubbing my still-bandaged palms on my thighs. It no longer hurt, and I could probably take the bandage off, but I was clinging to the only possession I had that wasn't my clothes.

When the alien continued to look at its little device, I knocked on the side of the cube, and when that did nothing, I pounded with both palms.

"What do you want from us?" I cried out.

When it didn't respond or look at me again, I started screaming, the desperation for answers washing over me in waves. It was the first time their behavior had changed, and still, we were rewarded with no additional information. The alien then moved on to one of the other girls and repeated the same process, checking its little screen and the girl in front of him but otherwise ignoring their attempts to get its attention.

I said nothing to the other girls about my suspicions. The way they treated us was strange. We obviously weren't guests, but we weren't cattle either.

From the sterile way they dealt with us, poking at us with probes and otherwise leaving us to our own devices, it felt like we were experiments.

The silence was getting to me, and I had started singing to myself to stop from going insane. I sang any song I could remember or repeated out loud lines from a movie or commercial that was stuck in my head because hearing my voice was better than waiting in the still silence for the clack of the food tray being dropped on the floor. I clung to that sound almost as much as I did the food that was delivered because it was all I had to remind me this was real.

They hadn't fed us our first meal of the day, and when it came time for our second, they approached the cubes, but none of them held trays of food. Instead, they were in groups, several holding something that looked like cattle prods.

They had finally come for us.

This time when they reached through the sides of the cubes, they reached for me, doing a strange hand gesture that was almost beckoning. They made a clicking noise of irritation when I refused to come into their open arms.

The silence I had known for days was broken by the shushing sound of the side of the cube opening, and a rush of fresh, ice-cold air engulfed the space around me. I backed against the rear wall as four of them entered the cube, their feet slapping loudly on the floor. But there was nowhere for me to go, and the aliens again were unconcerned with my struggles and screams, which now that the cubes were opened, echoed from all four corners of the room as the other girls' shrieks joined mine as we fought.

The hands of the alien spacesuits felt like the suckers on octopus legs, and with two aliens per woman, one on either side while a third stood menacingly behind us with the evil cattle prods, we were escorted from our cubes. Suddenly, the cubes felt like the safest place we could have been, and I wanted to be back inside, away from the aliens. At least in the cubes, they left us alone.

They dragged us from the cubes and into the main room.

Tori was giving them a run for their money, and with an angry shriek, the alien behind her jabbed her in the lower back with the prod. Her body stiffened, and she cried out in pain, but was much more subdued after that.

I shuddered, deciding as much as my mind was telling me to fight, maybe I should comply.

For now.

As we were moved through the room, I grabbed for Samara, the closest to me, and she reached for me. The brush of her hand was the most grounding thing I had felt in days, and I clung to that feeling of humanity as we were dragged apart. The girls' screaming subsided as we moved through a short hallway, and one by one, we were taken into separate rooms, the doors sliding closed with another quiet whoosh, ceasing all sound from the other side. Until it was only me and my screaming left, echoing around the hall.

My heart was pounding, and as I was dragged through a set of sliding doors, I started to hyperventilate. Mostly, I'd been able to maintain a level of numbness while in the cube because I was alone and not being touched. But the fear rushed back the second they grabbed me with their sucky, pockmarked suits, and all I could hear was my blood pounding in my ears and my breathing and panting full of terror. They paid no attention to me or my panic. I was strapped to a flat board in the middle of the room—plain white and cold like everything else on the ship.

After struggling uselessly against the binds that held my torso, wrists, thighs, and ankles for a few moments, I began muttering the Lord's Prayer, the only one I remembered from Sunday school.

Too much in shock to continue struggling, I stayed still, clamped to the table, and darted my eyes around the room wildly, trying to figure out what they were going to do and if there were any chance of escape. I could see none, and I swallowed back the bile rising in my throat.

With a buzzing sound, the table I was lying on began shifting, and my legs were forced to spread open and bend at the knees.

Oh God, no.

The screaming started then, coming from somewhere inside me that responded with pure terror. I didn't realize it was me until a split second after the sound began. I didn't stop even when my throat was raw, simply letting the sounds that escaped me turn from a high-pitched scream of terror into raspy sobs and pleads. The aliens approached me with another white instrument of some kind, spiraled and thick with a round nodule at the tip. It was almost two feet long, and my screams intensified. The aliens ignored me.

My cotton shorts and panties were cut away at the crotch with a small pen-sized instrument that emitted light and made no sound, the small fragments of fabric discarded. The aliens then approached me with their torture device.

As they got closer, the round nodule came into focus, and inside it was a swirling white substance and something that looked familiar. Once I placed it, I started crying anew, struggling against the binds, my tears so thick I couldn't see properly.

Tadpoles. They looked like tadpoles.

I could guess what it was for when they came level with me.

I was jerking from the strength of my sobs.

CHAPTER 5

ERICA

Seconds passed, and nothing happened.

I had scrunched my eyes closed, trying to pretend I was anywhere but here. Shit, I wanted to be back at school, being bullied and shoved into the locker room, locked inside overnight. I would be back with my ex, cowering in a back room as he pounded on the door while I hoped like hell the chair I had pushed under the doorknob would hold. I would even be back at my father's funeral, finding out my mother had already moved on with someone else before the disease even took my dad away.

Anywhere. But. Here.

Still, nothing happened.

The air was freezing against my crotch, but no one had touched me, and no instrument had been forced upon me.

I opened my eyes, one before the other, as if the slower I opened them, the more chance I had of waking and realizing this was all a nightmare. The aliens were all staring, without making a noise or moving, at my exposed pussy. I tried to close my legs but was unable to do so with the restraints, and my embarrassment quickly turned to rage when they continued to stare.

"What? Not what you paid for?" I screamed at them. One of them tilted its head in my direction, and I recoiled slightly. The first time I had been able to look directly into the panel on their face, I had seen only one sickly green eyeball with red veins and a pupil, staring back at me.

They started making noises, clicking and murmuring between them, indicating the instrument in their hands and then pointing between my legs.

Hope flared in me.

Maybe they had made a mistake and thought humans were different.

Maybe they would take us home.

The conversation between them escalated, and the noises became louder, screeching at each other as the sounds ricocheted off the walls. The one holding the torture wand threw it across the room and then turned and shoved hard at the alien next to him. They were fighting, still pointing between my legs.

One came up, angrily waving its arms about, holding the smaller white wand I had seen when I first was taken. It jammed it into my belly button again, and I cried out in pain. It maneuvered the tool, pressing hard, and I started screaming again, certain if it kept going like that, it would punch through my stomach with the blunt instrument. When it lowered its face to my belly, I tried to move away but had nowhere to go as it ran its sticky, suited fingers over my flesh, close to its face, inspecting. The others had fallen silent, and when the inspecting alien was finished with its work, it began talking. It was calm at first until the sounds from it rose in pitch and volume, and it pointed from my stomach to between my legs.

It seemed I was what they wanted inside but not outside.

I prayed they didn't try to cut me open to get inside.

They weren't happy with my body, and I could only guess what they had planned to do, and it sure seemed like they wanted to impregnate me. I started muttering to myself, whispering pleas and prayers that they would tire of us and let us go.

There was more fighting, and then the straps

were removed from my arms and legs. I tried to make a run for it, but the alien stayed steadfast on its feet when I shoved it, its low center of gravity meaning it was like trying to push a brick wall. The cattle prod was waved in front of my face, and I stilled, letting them roughly usher me toward the door I had entered through. We went down the same hallway, but instead of turning back into the room with the cubes, we continued straight before turning too many corners for me to count. When I started to lag with my steps, they'd poke me in the small of my back, and the two aliens gripping my arms would yank me forward.

This was not good.

The agitated sounds from the aliens increased as we walked, and we came to a junction in the hallway, the sounds increased even more as several groups of aliens converged in the area where the halls met. The other girls were there, looking equally as confused and frightened as I felt.

"What's going on?" Misha stammered, raising her voice to be heard over the yammering of the angry aliens.

"I have no idea." I paused, watching the aliens around us. They seemed unconcerned we were talking, and other than the ones holding our arms tight, they once again ignored us. "I don't think we're what they wanted."

"Does that mean we get to go home?" Samara

piped up.

"I don't know. I hope so."

But looking around at the aliens again, I wasn't so sure. Whatever they wanted us for evidently was not going to plan, and what was stopping them from simply tossing us out into space or killing us? They had no reason to take us back to Earth. If there was nothing stopping them from abducting us in the first place, I can't imagine there would be anything stopping them from getting rid of us.

I started to tremble and did my best to stop it as I noticed the other girls watching me. As I was the first one to be taken and was usually the initiator of conversations while in our cubes—when I noticed someone was in a slump—now I was apparently the one to be looked up to. I tried to wait until they were asleep to cry, being the strength I needed someone else to be for me.

But there was no one else.

There never was.

The chattering died down, and the aliens turned to face us. There was a brief pause before they started shuffling us forward again. This time in one large group, dozens of flat hands pressed against us and forced us to walk. When I reached out for Tori, my arm was slapped away.

"I think they're going to let us go!" Samara cried out. There was hope in her voice, and I don't know what about this situation made her so hopeful—she was apparently a positive person, even directly in the face of fear. A pang of pain stabbed in my chest at the idea I would probably never get to find out what sort of person she was beyond that.

I didn't want to be her reality check, not this time.

I didn't want to be the one who told her we were all about to die.

We were weeks into deep space, and for all I knew, they were simply going to shove us out of an air shoot and let us suffocate or freeze, blow up, or whatever happens when you're left in the vacuum of space without a suit. Why continue to feed and care for an experiment that didn't work?

We came to another white room, rounded, and the walls dotted with black circles at the aliens' head height, almost like windows. One of the aliens hit a panel by the door, and four oval pods moved forward out of the walls, small doors opening up to reveal a single seat inside each.

Oh shit.

I screamed, the other girls following suit. We all began fighting at once, trying to yank our arms from the aliens' grips and attempt to find an exit. But there were too many of them—more than I had even seen in the main room where we had been kept—and we were each shoved forward into a pod. By numbers and weight alone, they managed to push us, and the door of the pod closed the second I hit the seat. I pivoted in the small space and pounded my palm against the door. I could see through the small round window, but there were no controls inside that I could find, only the tiny uncomfortable seat.

They were going to dump us.

Still screaming, I pressed my face against the window seeing the other girls shoved into their seats. The pod jolted, and my nose hit the window as I cried out, falling back into the seat and holding my face, my hands coming away bloody. Mere seconds later, when I looked back up and out the window, I was shooting through space, and the spaceship—white, round, and sterile like the interior—was disappearing from view. My stomach lurched, and I desperately tried to keep my mouth shut, not wanting to vomit in the pod's small space.

The pod spun, and the blackness of the sky was replaced as a planet came into view, and whites of clouds spread across the sphere, then the greens of plants.

Was this Earth?

Had they indeed taken us back home?

My hope was stamped out when the pod continued to rotate, and a body of water came into clearer view—gray, the deep dark gray of an ocean. The sun, larger than I'm sure ours was, had a distinct orange tint to it. And the green definitely looked like a forest, but where were the cities? The civilization? There was nothing I could see. Where were the continents? Anything of recognizable shape?

This was *not* Earth.

Definitely *not* home.

We were going to crash land on an alien planet.

If I survived the fall, God knows what sort of life was waiting there for us. Were there more aliens waiting on the surface and ready to take us to labs to impregnate us with their giant tadpole sperm? To cut us open because their instruments on the ship hadn't worked? I dry-heaved a few times and scrambled around in the small space, trying to find anything that resembled a control panel.

The pod plummeted toward the planet, picking up speed as it flew. Shifting forward, I looked out the window again, pressing my face against the surface of the glass to try to locate the other pods. As I passed through some clouds, I lost sight of everything, but when I came out the other side, I cried out when I saw another pod. But it was tiny in the distance and moving away from me as fast as it was heading toward the surface. It disappeared over near the horizon and the gray line of the ocean. I just hoped whoever was in that pod didn't drown. Turning my head, I tried to find the other pods and found one slightly closer to me but moving farther away toward the purplish mountains before disappearing over the back of the peak.

Looking down, I was also heading for the mountains but not on the same side as the second pod I spotted. I seemed to be heading straight for the foot of the mountain, every second bringing the large rocks into clearer view.

Not only was I about to crash on an alien planet, I wasn't going to land anywhere near the other girls.

I'd be alone.

The third and final pod I located seconds later, and I kept it in sight as long as possible, but I had no idea which of the girls were in it. As it neared the surface, I cried out, thinking it was going to hit the ground and kill her. But seconds before impact, a large cushion-like appendage shot out, white and more solid than any parachute I'd ever seen. But it slowed the progress enough that I exhaled before the pod disappeared from my sight toward the opposite horizon as the other had gone, into a dense green area which I could only assume was a forest of some sort.

I was thankful we weren't going to end up as pancakes on the surface, but that was only part of our problems.

We would all be alone and miles apart.

I headed toward some mountains, and with a jolt, I realized my parachute must have released.

And as the view of the surface rushing toward me made my stomach lurch again, I closed my eyes.

CHAPTER 6

ILK

Another new species.

I had hoped it was over.

The last drop was over a year ago, and when the Moeks beamed up their supplies in payment for the abducted species, the containers were promptly dropped back to the surface, smashing open.

Empty.

The Ghaal were fed up with waiting, and the message was clear.

Bring us the females we seek, or no more fuel and supplies.

The Moek ship had left with an angry sweep over the island, churning up dust and ripping up trees in the wake of its power, and hadn't been seen since. I had never quite relaxed, but with every month that passed, I hoped the Moeks wouldn't be able to obtain more compatible females, and it would be over.

Originally, I'd thought the Moeks were nasty creatures like the Ghaal, but they too, were a dying species, just as desperate to rekindle their numbers. They would be on a search of their own for fertile females, and part of the deal was they were able to test the compatibility of those abducted, and if they didn't suit them, the Ghaal had a second shot.

Part of me suspected the Moeks intentionally created issues for the Ghaal for a while. Some of the species they dropped here were clearly not compatible for themselves or the Ghaal. Maybe they did this as a small act of rebellion to satiate part of their conscience because there was no way they didn't know the fate of the females they delivered here.

As I watched the units drop, beams of a bright white shot down around the other side of the mountain closer to the shore, collecting whatever it was they'd been promised from the Ghaal colony and bringing it to the safety of the ship.

The small units dropped from the sky as many others had before them and were always stopped from hitting the ground with giant wings that slowed their progress and dropped them gently to the surface of our planet.

Watching the units, I frowned—there were only four.

But the Ghaal worked in sixes—they always worked in sixes. I didn't understand. The pattern had been broken, which could only mean one thing—the species in these units were indeed the ones they had been seeking. They had to be. Maybe they couldn't get six or were so desperate it no longer mattered. It seemed strange—all their superstitions and workings were based around the number, so why abandon it now?

Desperation.

After years of different species being brought here against their will by the Moeks, populating our still-reviving planet with an assortment of other species which didn't belong together, these were the ones the Ghaal had been waiting for. Since the original lot didn't survive the experiments, they had sought and now successfully gained more—the ones with the pale hair, smooth, light skin, and that tuft of hair between their legs. The thick black hair was absent from their arms, spine, and legs as the Ghaal have.

The images of that female's mangled body still haunted me.

Before and since those females, when they seemed unable to get more, the Ghaal continued experimenting on every species the Moek would drop in their ever-increasing desperate attempts to find the right one. Each time was different, and once they got to our planet, every species behaved differently. Some were able to adapt and simply move on with their lives in the new terrain, separate or together, and made the most of where they were. Others panicked and disappeared before I was able to help, and they either perished or wound up in the hands of the Ghaal.

Neither was an option I wanted for them.

I tried to help where I could, but some species couldn't or wouldn't communicate. I suspected many were animals without self-awareness or intelligence enough to understand what had happened. On the rare occasion I recognized a like intelligence, most were too overcome with fear to communicate. I could only hope I got enough across to them to retain the one most important piece of information about this planet and my sole purpose for tracking down the new species.

Stay away from the Ghaal colony.

There had been several species I had been able to learn from, but their language was simplistic, and while I had been unable to maintain a conversation, I could only communicate enough to keep them safe from the colony. I could learn their language if they would let me, but it was a feat that required trust, and my appearance frightened most species.

With every single one of these misplaced species, even if they were frightened, I still attempted to steer them away from the colony at the base of the mountains near where I called home. For death would be better than getting into the Ghaals' hands. I had stationed myself near enough to the colony so I could keep an eye on them but far enough that over the years, hopefully, they had all but forgotten me and my kind existed.

Unlikely.

They hated us Synths with a seething rage. They blamed us for not helping to save them.

Perhaps they no longer cared. We had left them alone for so long I wondered if they were even aware we were directing new species away from them when we could. That was if we were lucky enough to be closer to the dropped units than the colony was.

One of the units, the last to release its wings, floated down near me. This, of course, would be the unit I would find. I moved immediately to investigate. I'd tracked the other units during their descent, and while only two of the other three had landed close to where my brothers were, hopefully, my brothers would find them before any Ghaal scouts did.

I could not go after them all, so I headed toward the nearest one first.

I never wanted this day to come, but knew

it was inevitable.

Perhaps this female I would be able to communicate with quickly, or at least she would let me get close enough to learn her language. I'd only encountered one once, and she was already dead before we found her. I knew nothing of their language or minds, and as with every encounter, I never wanted to frighten innocent species. The units were too small to hold any being of the same stature as me, and I was aware my presence was frequently alarming for them.

I was often lonely, and sometimes I wondered how my brothers were coping and how their chosen habitats had changed them.

Synths were adaptive. We learned, and without conscious thought, our bodies shifted to our environment and needs over time.

I had chosen the mountains as my home out of duty to protect others from the Ghaal colony, and my body had changed until I was almost a part of the mountains and the rocks, and now it would feel wrong to leave. Lanir was the closest to me, around the other side of the mountain. Another brother, Vitri, had chosen a forest to dwell in, and a fourth, Sahcor, was near the ocean. Two others—Eldich and Ryth—were farther away, covering as much of the island as we could. I could only imagine how their different environments had changed them. The part of me that was always keen to learn new information—to keep my brain young and virile—wanted to know what they looked like now and how they behaved. If only for curiosity's sake.

And because I missed them.

Stepping over and around the rocks and boulders, a path I could walk without sight if I needed to, I found the unit wedged between two boulders, having not made it all the way to the ground. I kept my distance and simply watched. It would open soon, and the latest species to come to our planet would emerge. I did not want to frighten her immediately, so I hid. If I stayed still amongst the rocks, I would be almost invisible.

The unit opened, and the being was exposed, sinking back into the seat and clinging to it. She was so small, and after a moment, she moved cautiously, sticking her head out of the opening and scanning the area, breathing unevenly. Every breath was mounted with fear, and I could smell it in the air between us. My chest ached for her, knowing she would never know her own home again. I had seen this many times—too many to count—and it hurt every time. I could not save them all.

But this one, she was brought here with the Ghaal *knowing* she was compatible. More than anything, I would not let her be harmed.

Her eyes, small and bright, swept right over me. I blended in with the stones around me, in color and texture, and I watched her back, hidden. My nostrils flared as I sniffed the air, her feminine scent strong even under what I assumed was weeks of grime and sweat. An ache ran through my chest again to think what she had already been through before landing, and now she would be faced with more challenges.

Her eyes were quite attractive, even though rounded with fear. A deep brown, the same shade as the long hair that grew only from her head, not the same as the light yellowish hair of the dead female Lanir and I had found. Maybe she was from a different colony? How strange that should be the only place she should have hair growing was on the top of her head. Did she also have the tuft between her legs? I wondered the purpose of it and why they had evolved that way. Hopefully, I would get the chance to ask her. In my original form, I looked like my creators with a line of course fur that ran up my spine and down the back of my arms, which would raise and make me appear larger than I was when angry or frightened. But as I am now, I had, similar to the female, long hair, except mine was of a dark purple which I pulled together into a braid and left it to trail down my back.

Her gaze fell upon the ground, and she squeaked when she realized she was not quite on the surface. Should I help? I was unsure. She seemed frightened, so small, and my presence alone might startle her.

When she emerged farther, small hands gripped the sides of the unit, and I stilled.

Unmistakably and irresistibly female.

Two petite mounds upon her chest presented themselves under the flimsy rags, an excuse for clothing she wore to cover her body. The curves of her hips and legs became visible as she straightened halfway out of the unit and surveyed the distance before looking back to the ground and trying to judge if she could make the jump. I tried unsuccessfully not to take in every line of her body I could see, and I held back a possessive growl that threatened to rumble through my chest.

Before the Ghaal began kidnapping, they tried to synthesize a species for breeding—my brothers and I—and seeing this female brought forth an instinct I had long kept buried.

We were *made* to breed—it lived in our veins, in our DNA.

Absent from females, I could ignore the instincts.

But now she was here...

The core of me, which desired to claim and mate, was stirred by her scent.

I pressed down the urge.

Those rags she was wearing would do no good in these mountains. Her skin looked soft and fragile, so she would need much better clothing. I could make her more suitable clothes.

I took another deep, steadying breath as her scent overcame me again. I didn't need to continue to stare at her and take deep lungfuls of air to determine she was female, but once I got a hint of her scent, it was difficult to stop myself from gasping for more air, hoping to catch a whiff of her on the wind. She wasn't clean, but beyond the scent of dirt and soiling was her female scent—soft and delicate like her skin.

Almost all the beings dumped on this planet were female. However, gender was not the same between all species, so this was not always the case.

But looking her over again, my chest ached for her. She was in terrible danger. I wanted to tell her and sweep her up in my arms to protect her.

The similarities were not lost on me between the female being, the Ghaal, and therefore myself. Two legs, two arms, two eyes. She had one more finger and toe than I did on each hand and foot—five instead of four—and hers were many times smaller than mine. I was molded after my makers, and this small female may not have the harsh gray skin tone of the Ghaal or the orange-tinted irises and flat wide palms. Her skin may be soft and subtle and not etched with the semblance of scales from a long-lost ancestral trait, but she was similar enough for me to realize the Ghaal was right—she was a match for them. They'd desire to breed with her, either manually or artificially.

And I couldn't let that happen.

If the Ghaal saw her, they would take her. So, I must take the risk of frightening her in order to protect her from a fate worse than death.

I must protect her.

This female was in danger, and the only thing standing between her and the Ghaal was me.

CHAPTER 7

ERICA

So my stupid pod couldn't even make it to the surface. Once the door had silently slid open, disappearing into the sides of the pod as though it was never there to begin with, and I had let go of the breath I'd been holding, I leaned over the edge to find I was at least six feet from the ground. I'm sure I could jump it and not injure myself under any normal circumstances, but the ground looked hard and uneven, made entirely of rocks and boulders of a grayish-purple color, dark and dappled in places, spots of white on others in almost a marbled effect.

All right, I could admire the colors of the rocks once I found a way to the ground.

Scanning the horizon, I was met with imposing mountains that stretched around to my right, and to my left. If I were to walk far enough, there appeared to be a forest where I had seen one of the other girls disappear. But it was small and distant, and I had no idea if there would be civilization beyond or near it or how many days it would take to reach it.

Pausing to listen for anything that might sound familiar—birds, vehicles, literally anything—the background noise was a broken hum I didn't recognize. Possibly bird calls, but it didn't sound appealing. I think I could hear running water, maybe a river, and momentarily I was excited, but that was dashed by the incredibly real possibility if it were indeed running liquid, it could be poisonous, and I would never know.

The panic threatened to overwhelm me, and I kept it down with a few deep breaths, swallowing against the bile in my throat. *Hey, at least I wasn't suffocating. Yay. Point to me.* Now I could starve to death instead or take my chances on some unknown plant and hope it didn't kill me or give me hives or super diarrhea. Fun.

I missed my bed.

Hell, I even missed the stupid soundless cube on the ship. At least they fed us.

Glancing down again at the ground, I decided my best bet was to dangle from the pod to lessen the drop. I had no shoes, so at least I'd have a decent grip, but I didn't like my chances of not rolling my ankle. Or worse.

Turning around, I backed my butt out of the doorway, thankful no one was around to see as I still had a damn hole in the crotch of my shorts, not that the shorts would be covering much anyway. They were designed for sleeping, not for climbing over rocks. One of the legs of my shorts I had almost ripped entirely off to use to clean myself after I used the bathroom, along with a strip from my top. I simply couldn't stand the idea of being dirty, and it's left me with a crop top and half short-half bikini cotton monstrosity with a cutout crotch.

Gripping onto the edge of the pod, I lowered one foot outside. Slightly emboldened, I dropped my other leg and tried to keep as much control as possible as I lowered myself until I was dangling from my fingertips.

Right now, all that was left to do was to let go.

Let go.

Let go, Erica.

Just let go of the alien pod.

Let go of your only safety from terrible weather and strange creatures.

Just. Let. Go.

Fuck.

My fingers were starting to ache, but fear was taking over, and as my hands grew numb, I simply couldn't bring myself to let go of the damn pod. When it shifted slightly between the two boulders, I squealed in fright and clung to it harder.

Nope. Fuck this. I'm going back up.

Unfortunately for me, I had fuck all upper body strength, and no matter how much I swore and kicked around, I couldn't pull myself back into the pod.

When the ground started to tremble, I cried out in fright, doubling my effort to get back into the pod. Either there was an earthquake, or I was about to be eaten by a T-Rex, but either way, I was getting back into the damn pod and staying there. There has to be some sort of control panel somewhere, right? Maybe I missed it, and it was hidden behind a fake wall or something or inside the chair. I was certain if I tore the entire thing apart, I'd find a way to control it.

My fingers were slipping as sweat formed on my hands. I was torn between moments of trying to rally myself to finally let go and drop to the ground or attempting to pull myself back up into the pod.

Because if I needed any extra motivation, it was the realization that the trembling of the ground was definitely approaching footsteps. The more I protested and squealed, the faster they stomped toward me, and with a final cry, I let go of the pod.

But I never hit the ground.

Two large hands encircled my waist, and I balled

my hands into fists, pounding them against the hands around my waist before I shoved my fists near my mouth to stifle the screams. The alien turned me around to face it, and wide-eyed, I couldn't look away. But I guess I'm more of a coward than I thought I was because I got one glimpse of a muscled gray chest, the same color as the boulders, and bright green eyes gazing at me curiously from a large face with flatter features than me, giving the illusion he was made of stone. *Because he had to be an illusion, right?*

Only a glimpse before my vision grayed, and I let out a weak protest of, "Nooo…" before I passed out.

CHAPTER 8

ILK

She was unconscious.

In the end, I had frightened her so much she had put herself into a sleep state to protect herself from the panic. The tiny female had tried to lower herself to the ground and, in her terrified state, she flailed and squealed and had not let go of the unit straightaway. I wanted to tell her she was quite close to the ground, and if she had let go, she would have been fine, but I thought perhaps a shout would startle her enough to cause an injury. When she had stretched out, her arms above her head and flimsy rags no longer covering her stomach and back very well, she looked even smaller and more fragile than

I had originally thought.

As I turned her gently to lie across my arms in her fright-sleep, I traced her skin with my fingers—a pleasant pale color. The hair on her head was soft, and I huffed out a breath making it shift. It would be no good for making a nest, nor to provide material for ropes or sewing as mine did, and it was too long to raise when she wanted to make herself appear bigger to predators, so I was no closer to understanding its purpose. Unless it was to attract a mate because, for that purpose, it was working extremely well. I was trying hard to resist the urge to take a lock in my hand and inhale its scent, certain it would smell like her—gentle and feminine. I had encountered many females of many species, but none who looked so similar to me while still being so entirely different, and she stirred parts of me I had ignored for so long I'd almost forgotten they existed. But also, few species had appeared quite so vulnerable. I could see nothing on her she could use as a defense since she didn't have hard skin or quills, and she had no claws or sharp teeth.

She was so delicate.

Without me, this female was defenseless.

Her planet must be safe because she was not built for survival outside.

But knowing about her planet was not important right now.

I would take her home, keep her warm and fed

until I could explain to her the dangers of this planet and teach her what she needed to know to survive. Perhaps she would like to find the others who were dropped off with her. I didn't know anything about her kind, but they may prefer to live in packs than alone.

Either way, I would help.

Moving across the boulders, I made my way back to the cave I had called home for the past many years and fashioned a small bed for her from furs and animal skin. The female didn't need many, the fur from the oarke was several times larger than me, and she needed only a corner to be wrapped around her before she was tucked in and warm.

I sat and watched her.

It would seem an invasion to link with her mind and learn what I could of her language while she was in this state, but if I didn't, she would unlikely be able to understand me and might frighten again.

I didn't know what to do.

Standing, I moved to the cave entrance and shifted a boulder in front of it, feeling a pang of guilt as I did so. I did not want to keep her prisoner, but it was imperative she know and stay away from the Ghaal colony. They would have seen the units drop and would surely be aware these were the females they had waited so long for. Perhaps it might even be best if we traveled, not staying in one area too long.

I would need to consult the female if she was intelligent enough. Crouching near her, I studied the rags of her clothes. The stitching was fine and intricate, definitely made by machine like the Ghaal did in previous generations. The pattern was colorful and strange but faded. These were not the clothes of a savage species—this female was intelligent. I wondered how far her species' technology had progressed. Had they mastered space travel?

If I were a being without conscience or care, I would simply invade her mind now. Perhaps she wouldn't care, but I knew nothing of her culture. No. The risk was too great. I couldn't shatter her trust in me as my first act. I needed to ask her permission somehow. I could only wait until she woke and hoped she'd let me touch her mind later. Only a moment would be enough for me to get the basics of her language. A little longer, and I could learn all the words she knew, and with a night and a day, I could obtain all her memories too.

Synths were given this ability so we could learn quickly and adapt because our makers did not have to waste time teaching us things as you would a youngling. We adapted the skill and evolved it, as we did with everything. My appearance had only changed after many years in my environment, but my strength and the hardening of my skin occurred after a few days of being out of the colony and living in the wild.

The female stirred, and I moved back slightly so I was still near her but not so close she would startle when she opened her eyes. But she did not wake. Growing concerned, I fetched my water bag, holding it to her mouth and pressing slightly to dampen her lips. Her tongue darted out and found the liquid running across those pinkish lips. They looked so soft and strange that I wanted to touch them. Ghaals had lips, but they were thinner and almost without color of their own, no different from the grayish tone of their skin. I have lips, but mine are not soft nor pink, but over time of being in the mountains had hardened and changed color like the rest of my skin. I pressed the bag to the female's mouth again, squeezing it a bit harder. The liquid flooded her mouth, and she swallowed gratefully, licking her lips again, her eyelids fluttering.

Her tongue was also small and pink.

Instinct stirred, and I couldn't stop myself.

I reached forward to touch it as it darted out, and when my finger made contact with the pink muscle, she woke, and her eyes flew open. She sat up abruptly, cried out, and scooted away from me across the cave's floor until she was curled up near the rear wall.

"Please don't be frightened," I murmured, doing my best to keep my voice soothing for the small female. She only squeaked in response and cowered farther against the wall. When I stepped toward her, she held her hands in front of her as though they were a barrier between us. She spoke then, saying something to me. I did not understand her words, but her voice was high and panicked, and I could only assume she was terrified, and this was not how she normally sounded. The female had appeared to be talking to herself when she was hanging from the unit, and her voice then was slightly deeper and exceedingly pleasant to listen to. The fear in the tone now hurt my heart, so I stopped and then stepped back.

She watched me wearily, lowering one hand and then closing her fist until she pointed at me with only one finger. "Staee!"

The word was strange, and I attempted to repeat it back to her, reaching out to touch her finger with mine. "Ssstaee."

Her eyes widened, and she kept her hand outstretched until my finger was a whisper from hers, then withdrew her hand with another squeak. Her hands were so tiny I could have wrapped both of them up in one of mine.

But her breathing had slowed, and I kept my distance as her fear, while still present, ebbed away slightly. She watched me for a long time, and when I made no move to get closer, she stood slowly, dragging her tiny hands up the cave wall behind her and never shifting her gaze from mine. Keeping close to the wall, she followed its curve around to the entrance, where the light from the sun was visible through a crack at the top. She looked away from me only long enough to inspect the boulder I had rolled in front of the exit, and then she attempted to move it.

I couldn't help it and chuckled at her attempts. She spun around and glared at me and then returned to her try to shift the stone again, shoving her shoulder and hands against it and grunting. When it wouldn't move, the female turned back to face me, one hand poised on her delicate hip and the other pointing at the stone.

"Mewv eet," she demanded. I cocked my head at her. "Lemme awt!"

I could only assume she wanted to exit, so I straightened my back and posture to show her I wasn't moving. Lifting a hand to my head, I then indicated her head, withdrawing my hand from the space between us when she shrunk away. After a beat, I did the gesture again, trying to show her I could merge our minds.

Did she have that ability on her planet?

Would she know what I was trying to show her?

Maybe I would have no choice but to show her.

I didn't want to force her, but if we could communicate, it would make this easier on us. She had no idea the danger she was in and how valuable she was to the remnants of a vicious race. The female needed protection.

I moved toward her, but no matter how slow I tried to approach, she shrieked and shrunk away from me. In her scramble, she tripped over the furs and landed on her back. I groaned with alarm and rushed to her as she released a startled yelp when she landed. She was so fragile, even hitting the hard floor of the cave might be too much for her. *How easily did her body break?* I didn't know. Her skin didn't seem hard enough to protect her from injury.

On her back with her legs spread, she was exposed to me. The thin rags that covered her body were ripped open at the crotch, and I stilled.

Dread filled me because looking at her confirmed my suspicions that she was *exactly* what the Ghaal would want.

Her scent mingled in the air, and a growl rumbled through my throat.

No. I told myself I mustn't touch her. I had evolved, and I was no longer the being created for breeding I had started as.

But I could smell her, and her cunt called to me.

Lunging at her, she screamed and scrambled against the furs to get away from me as I placed a hand on her soft stomach and held her down, grabbing her ankle with my other hand when she started to kick at me.

I groaned. Her scent was intoxicating.

I had driven down the urges long ago that rose in

me now. By choice, I had attempted to exile that part of myself as all of us Synths had. Being created to breed, despite our intelligence, we were still beings fueled by instinct. Even being close to each other was difficult for the brief time we lived together, still learning control and forcing ourselves not to allow half of us to change to female and give in to our desires to mate. Calling each other brothers helped, although, in reality, we shared no such relationship.

But this female was bringing it back—the instinctual side that made a beast of me was being awoken. I groaned as my nostrils flared, and she whimpered. My grip on her ankle increased, and my mind flooded with images I shouldn't be having. It would be so easy to take her and sink my cock into her waiting warmth right now.

I didn't want to scare the female, but she was so perfect. So soft and gentle. The female needed my protection from the wilderness and the Ghaal. She needed me even if she didn't know it. I thought of the other units and wondered if their occupants had survived. Hopefully, my brothers would find and care for them as I would this female before the Ghaal got to them.

Maybe she didn't need to go looking for them and could stay here with me.

There were billions of planets in the galaxies. How long had it taken for a suitable species to be dropped in the units? For them to find the first of the females like these? I had lost count.

And here she was.

It pained me that she was frightened of me. I wanted to show her that we weren't so different, that beyond the stone-like exterior of my skin that had only adapted due to my living conditions, I wasn't so different from her. The Synths' adaptation abilities weren't a choice, it was how we are. We could speed up the reaction or slow it down, but we couldn't stop it. Perhaps over time, if she stayed with me, I would appear less repulsive to her.

But now, all I wanted to do was touch her.

Just one touch.

Because if she was compatible with the Ghaal, then she was compatible with me too. Thoughts of breeding and having a family I had long forgotten and given up on came to the forefront of my mind.

I reached out and ran my finger between the folds of her cunt, and her scent intensified, drawing another agonized growl from my lips. Her terrified whimper changed into a squeak, and she bucked her hips when I hit the tiny nub at the top between the lips of her sweet cunt. She was responding to me, perhaps through touch alone, or maybe my pheromones had already started filtering through the cave to her.

Another part of me I couldn't help. If I became

aroused, I would release the pheromones designed to attract the one I wished to mate with further, to put them in a frenzy of breeding once they wanted it. It was not a drug but enough of an aphrodisiac for their response to be strengthened and magnified many times if they wished to mate.

Frowning, I gently rubbed the little nub again, and she moaned, finishing with a whimper. I shuddered at the sound, and sliding my finger down between her lips again, I poised my finger at the entrance to her cunt. She was so tiny, she would be so incredibly tight.

My cock ached at the thought.

No.

No, I can't do this to her.

She is frightened.

I'm *not* an animal.

Wrenching myself away from her, I moaned at the urges shuddering through my body, and turning my back, adjusting my loincloth to cover myself. I didn't want her to think I could hurt her or take her in a way she didn't want. She needed to trust me if I were to help and protect her. The female needed to feel safe with me.

Standing, I moved to the entrance of the cave and, with a heave, shifted the boulder. She watched me with narrowed eyes, those beautiful brown irises twinkling in the newly revealed sunlight. She scampered to her feet and as she passed, I grabbed her, hating the way she pulled away from my grip.

Lifting a fur from the floor, I shoved it into her hands. The female stopped struggling and took the fur, watching me with a frown as I let her go. She eyed me for a moment longer, but with another look at the cave opening, she ran off, clutching the small fur to her chest.

CHAPTER 9

ERICA

A lot of strange things had happened over the past few weeks, but that had to be at the top of the list. The large alien on this planet stopped me from hitting the ground after I escaped from the pod and had then taken me prisoner for a brief period.

I struggled to figure out if he was a good or bad guy, but maybe things weren't always so clear—he could be both. He could think he was doing the right thing and do the wrong thing in my eyes. Maybe the alien version of what was the right thing was not the same as mine. Maybe he was like a caveman and simply thought bonking me on the head and dragging me to his cave made us husband and wife.

I needed to get out of there.

I was tired of being held captive and scared.

I needed time to think.

Then he'd shoved a bunch of fur at me, and on instinct, I ran. But now I rubbed the fur against my face. It was incredibly soft, and I wished I had gotten another one from him.

I couldn't get the look of fascination on his face when he saw my pussy out of my mind. He'd touched me and quickly located my clit with a reaction I was unable to suppress. *Hell, a random stone alien man had located my clit faster than most of my ex-boyfriends!*

I was still scared. Of course I fucking was. I was stranded on an alien planet with no way to communicate or survive, and then to top it off, I'd been turned on by an alien who looked almost like a gargoyle.

This was a confusing day.

He wasn't entirely ugly, I suppose, once the initial shock of him had worn off. His skin was the same shade of grays and purples as the stones that littered the bottom of this mountain. He had a longish face, sharp features, and a large flat forehead. His nose had jagged edges, and on a human, I would have assumed it'd been broken several times. He was huge like a goddamn giant, maybe seven feet, with a barrel-like chest that was as hard as the stone he seemed to be made from. He looked like a sculpture, a work of art of sheer masculinity, but massive enough to be incredibly intimidating. The long, deep-purple braid he kept was flung over his shoulder and tied with a simple leather strap.

Gargoyle seemed an apt description to me.

But the way he had touched me, so gently, with a tenderness I hadn't experienced in years, and least of all expected from *him.* And on top of that, the *sound* he'd made when I couldn't contain my moan was like an animal, like he *craved* me. He smelled like heaven when I'd only expected him to smell of soil and nature, but there was something beyond that—a musky, smoky scent that made my head light and my eyelids flutter.

And hell, it made me want to buck my hips toward his wandering hand, not pull away.

But he'd recoiled and shuffled back from me as though I was a temptation to him, and I supposed there was something gallant about that.

My thoughts were on the border of trying to figure out what to do next when I was snatched from behind. It was my gargoyle alien man, and I screamed and struggled, not in the mood to be taken back to the prison cave this soon. Was this a game to him? Let me run, then capture me again? But all he did was spin me around and point me in the opposite direction I had been heading. His large flat forehead was curved with a frown, and he pointed behind himself, then to me, and growled.

"Alrighty," I mumbled, ignoring him and walking back toward the base of the mountains. When he snatched me up again, I simply said, "Oh, for fuck's sake." As he spun me around once again, he repeated the action, pointed to the base of the mountain over the ridge, then at me, and growled. Okay, so I guess he didn't want me to go that way. Maybe it was his territory, and I wasn't welcome or something. Whatever.

"Take it easy, big guy," I muttered before heading in the direction he had pointed me.

After a handful of steps, I turned back. The gargoyle was watching me but making no move to follow. Huffing out a breath, I headed straight toward a small group of trees. I wasn't even sure what I was looking for. Help, perhaps? I guess I had somewhat just left that behind, although his first move had been to trap me in a cave.

Now I was more confused than ever.

But I felt I'd made enough of a scene trying to get out of that damn cave that now I was too embarrassed by what the gargoyle thought of me, and I was going to at least try to get some exploring done.

Yep, I cared what the stone alien thought of me, but not sure what that said about me. My mind was a jumble as I walked. Do I continue to go on and look for help, or do I go back to the stone alien? Should I try to find the other girls? I scanned the distance, the nearest pod I had seen went behind the mountain, but the idea of traipsing over a strange mountain was more intimidating than walking a straight line to a forest. But it looked like it would take days to reach the tree line, and I had no food, shelter, or water.

The gargoyle had water.

Fuck.

Angrily, I kicked a stone, cursing when it hurt like hell. Continuing to grumble, I pulled the fur he had given me around my shoulders and continued toward the small patch of trees. At least, they looked like trees to me. All I could hope was they weren't giant teeth of some mega alien Venus flytrap. I had no experience surviving in the wild on Earth, let alone on a strange planet.

With no plan and no idea what I was looking for or where I was headed, hopelessness started to overwhelm me.

Scrap that. The hopelessness *had* overcome me.

I dropped to my knees, and a dry sob raked through my body, followed by another. Within seconds, I was a crying mess on my side, tucked my knees up to my chest, pulled the fur over my head, and let the emotions consume me because I needed this and had nothing else to do. I'd been taken from my home in the middle of the night, kept captive, probed and prodded, and then abandoned on a strange planet. Then I'd been grabbed by a *different*—albeit much nicer—alien, and I had no fucking idea what I was supposed to be doing now.

Fuck.

Fuck!

"Fuck!" I screamed again and again until it was just a wordless scream against the ground. Pulling the fur over my head farther, I screamed until my throat was raw and then sobbed until I couldn't breathe. I had no idea how long I stayed there, but eventually, the sobs subsided, and I lay curled up in a ball under the fur a nice alien had given me and merely rocked for a while.

Clearing my throat, I said, "Okay, Erica, time to toughen the fuck up."

Unrolling from my ball of despair, I stood, keeping my new fur wrapped around my shoulders and pulling the ends together to tie them in a knot, making myself a dark teal cape. Looking down, there was nothing I could do about the state of my clothes, so I would simply need to deal with them as they were.

Time to explore these trees.

My plan—search for signs of civilization—and the trees were as good a place to start as any, especially since the gargoyle wouldn't let me go farther into the base of the mountains. For a moment, I wish I had learned his name, then realized I had no way to ask him, so he would simply need to remain the gargoyle-esque stone alien man in my head.

Sighing, I headed toward the trees.

Once the ground changed from the boulders and rocky edges, it shifted into larger and flatter rocks that were easier to walk on, although a little warm on my feet from being under the bright orange sun. Looking up, it was high in the sky, so I'm guessing it was around midday, assuming time and orbit worked the same on this planet. Since I had nothing else to go on, I might as well make my assumptions.

Despite the sun, there was a chill in the air, but it wasn't entirely unpleasant. When I reached the trees, I studied them, hesitant to touch anything. They looked to be made of feathers, tall and thin and opening up to a wide fan brush-like head. As I watched, tiny creatures flitted in and out of the off-white brush top. I squinted, trying to see what they looked like beyond the blurs they presented as they darted around but couldn't get a fix on them. The humming I had heard earlier was louder here, so it seemed the sound was coming from something resembling birdlife, after all. *Neat.*

I moved in and around the trees, but my sense of uneasiness grew as time went on, and I found myself hesitant to shift too far away from the gargoyle and his cave, instead circling and making sure I never lost my bearings. I searched through the scarce woods, none of the trees close enough together to block out my view of the mountain base, but I found nothing resembling water or food, and as the hours passed, my stomach started to growl. I hadn't eaten anything since the last meager meal provided by our capturers.

Glancing at the forest in the distance again, I trembled. I could assume it was a forest—a deep green haze against the horizon—but who knows? And without food and water, there was no way I'd be able to make it.

I had no choice.

Turning around, I headed back to the cave.

CHAPTER 10

ERICA

The gargoyle was ambling around near his cave entrance, and I snuck between the boulders, unwilling to announce my return just yet. For some reason, I still cared about what he thought of me, and I didn't want him to think I was weak because I came back so soon or that I was crazy for making a fuss in the first place and then returning almost immediately. In my defense, he had kept me captive. Although it still shouldn't matter what he *thought* of me. This was a life-or-death situation.

Maybe if I went up to him and asked, he would give me some more water.

Or maybe he would knock my head off.

Staying hidden, I watched him for a while.

When the sun had moved across the sky toward the horizon over the forest, he grabbed a bag that looked to be made of some sort of animal hide, along with the water bag he had shared with me earlier, and headed out across the flat plains of the rocks. *Fuck yeah, he was going to get some food and water, so all I needed to do was follow him, and I'd be set.*

Keeping behind the taller rocks, I slipped between them whenever his back was turned. Any sound created by my movement was hidden by the casual pounding of his heavy feet across the stone. When he came to the edge of the rocks where they tapered out into a grassy field like the one I had walked over to get back here, he stopped and dropped to his knees. Placing his bags next to him, he shoved his large hands into the soil, pulling out a patch of grass, roots, and dirt all in one. The grass was a pale wispy yellow, as though it was dying, but it looked soft enough in the way it brushed against his hands in the breeze. I found myself watching his hands, studying how his fingers were more squared at the end, not to mention he had only four of them, including his thumb. Remembering the way he touched me, I wondered what it would feel like if he hadn't stopped and pushed his thick finger inside me.

Fuck, concentrate on the food, woman, not the

way his shoulders rolled as he dug in the soil.

He was cleaning something, and I had to blink rapidly to focus on what he was doing. Attached to the roots of the grass were nodules that were almost completely clear, and as I watched, he brushed the soil off one and popped it in his mouth. He seemed happy with this and filled the bag with the root berries before standing again.

All right, root berries. I'll come back for those.

But I wanted to know where the water was.

He walked slowly, a casual amble, and I supposed he could take all the time he wanted. But I was thirsty, my mouth dry and uncomfortable every time I tried to lick my lips. I wanted to tell him to hurry up, but I kept hidden in case he wouldn't welcome me back.

After making his way in between the larger boulders, he reached up, lifted the water sack high, and scooped across the top of a rock.

Great, the water was up high.

After he had left the area, I moved to the boulder that apparently contained water on top of it. Standing next to it, I had to crane my neck. It was easily eight feet high, and there was no way I could climb it without slicing up my feet.

Cursing, I moved back to the grassy field. Hopefully, the root berries would quench my thirst. I made sure to keep out of sight, but the gargoyle was moving toward his cave, the heavy footfalls keeping me updated as to where he was. Well, with any luck that meant he wouldn't be able to sneak up on me at any point.

Crouching in the grassy field, I copied as I had seen him do and scooped up a handful of soil, pulling up a dozen root berries. Brushing the soil off, I sniffed at the berry. Just because it was safe for him to eat didn't mean it would be for me too. But what choice did I have?

Closing my eyes and thinking a quick prayer, I popped it in my mouth.

It was sweet, a burst of pleasant flavor that soothed my mouth and throat. It was almost like a balloon with a thin outer layer that popped when I pressed it between my tongue and the roof of my mouth, releasing the oily liquid inside. I hummed and had another and another, shifting so I was sitting cross-legged and enjoyed my feast.

I contemplated digging up more and carrying them around, but where was I going to go? The cave wasn't far away. I wondered if the alien man was interested in trying to communicate. Now that I wasn't so hungry and thirsty and my head was clearer, I remembered he had tried to mimic my words before. Maybe we could talk more if I taught him.

It was worth a shot.

I walked back to the cave, and when the rocks started to become more unstable, I was forced to take a pathway between two large, high boulders. As I came around them, a small water bag was resting on a flat area I couldn't have missed, waiting for me.

The stone alien man knew I was following him.

Damn, and I thought I was being so cautious.

When I got back to the cave, he was waiting, sitting by the entrance and leaning against the side of the mountain, and I think he *smiled* at me. There definitely was a lopsided grin. It was goofy and, in a weird way, kind of cute.

Okay, maybe I needed some sleep as well since I obviously wasn't thinking straight.

Cute gargoyle, bah.

I held up the water sack in a toast and smiled at him, and he continued to watch me, not responding even when I stood in front of him. He still didn't move, so I sat down, not close enough he could reach me, but close enough I could watch his face.

"Hello," I said. He stared at me. "Um…" I didn't have the faintest idea how to begin communication. "My name is Erica. What's yours?"

He said nothing but was still smiling. Okay, too complicated. I needed to simplify things.

Come on, Erica. You've seen movies.

I pointed to my chest. "Erica." I then pointed to him and waited.

And waited.

"Come on… I know you can talk!"

The edge of his lip curved. It was a smirk, almost like he was messing with me. All right, cheeky gargoyle alien who gave me water, found my clit, and has a sense of humor, time for you to stop making me think nasty thoughts I shouldn't be having.

"Okay, wise guy, I've got *all* day, so you might as well talk to me." I tried again. "Erica." I pointed to myself with a sharp jab toward my chest, then an equally as frustrated point at him.

"Ilk."

"Ah! He speaks!" I threw up my arms, and he smirked again. "You think you're so funny, huh? Ilk, is it?" I couldn't quite say it like he did with a little click at the end of the K, but I did my best. "Ilk." I pointed to him. "Erica." To me.

"Errrica."

"Right! Good work." His voice was gravelly and deep but not unpleasant, and while he dragged out the R and added a little click to the C, I thought it was close enough and quite good for a first try. I couldn't help but think of the screeching language of our kidnappers and how much more pleasant Ilk's rumbling voice was. Maybe his mouth was formed differently than mine, and he couldn't pronounce things the same. My eyes raked over his body from his large chest and shoulders down to where he wore only a loincloth and then down over his muscular legs to fur-lined boots.

Ilk seemed pleased with my praise of his pronunciation and was not at all bothered when I took a moment to glance at his body. When I returned my gaze to his face, his eyes were staring right into mine. We simply looked at each other for a moment. Maybe he was studying my features as much as I was his.

The sun dipped over the line of distant trees, the burning orange visible on the horizon. With the dusk came an abrupt wave of exhaustion that started in my shoulders and made my body sag. This was a lot, and everything had caught up with me. I tried to stifle my yawn, and Ilk's eyes widened slightly. He was on his feet in an instant and moved back into the cave.

"Shit." Had I offended him with my yawn? For all I knew, a yawn here was a declaration of war. "Ilk?" He didn't come back out, so I slowly followed him. He had made a fire, and there was a dull glow lighting the cave. The effect was warm and cozy, and it was made better by the fact Ilk was to the side adjusting a pile of furs into a bed.

He stood, his large head almost scraping the top of the cave, and pointed to the furs.

"Is that for me?" I asked.

"Errrica. Newp."

I had no idea what *newp* was, but I could guess, and at this stage, I was too tired to argue further. "I sure hope you mean *sleep.*" I made my way to the furs, undoing the knot around my neck which was holding the fur he had given me around my shoulders. I paused before sitting and again before lying down. Ilk looked pleased and folded the edge of the furs over. When I lifted my arm, I was hit with my own smell, and my nose crinkled. "Fuck, is that what I smell like? God, I'm so sorry, Ilk." He tilted his head when I said his name but said nothing. "Is there any way I can wash?" He still watched me, and I glanced around. I pointed to the water bag on the floor and then mimed showering and washing under my arms. "Wash."

"Hucna," he rumbled.

"I mean, maybe?" I repeated the motion, and Ilk nodded, picking up the water sack and grabbing a rag from the floor. He offered them to me. Damn, I guess he was smarter than I gave him credit for. He may look like a gargoyle, but I shouldn't assume anything about his intelligence.

Or how dangerous he could be.

Soaking the rag, I wiped away most of the grime and dirt from my face and body. I made quick work of it because Ilk wouldn't turn away and continued to smile that lopsided grin at me. I washed my torso and under my clothes only briefly. I threw the dirty rag outside the cave and quickly glanced at Ilk to make sure I hadn't offended him. I still wasn't clean, but it was better. Tomorrow maybe I would try to find a way to ask him if there was a river or lake I could bathe in.

Or a shower. *One could hope, I guess.*

I settled into the furs, and Ilk pulled them around me. "Newp," he said.

"Newp," I repeated.

Ilk seemed pleased.

I hoped he stayed that way and I didn't overstay my welcome.

I was asleep almost instantly.

CHAPTER II

ILK

Sleep, I told her, and she did.

Erica came back to me, and she was exhausted. It was endearing the way she had followed me earlier, moving in and around the boulders in an attempt at stealth. But she was clumsy, and despite her small stature, I heard her coming before I saw her. I had guessed she followed me out of hunger, so I sought out the simplest food for her to gather and moved slower through the terrain so she could keep up. While I preferred meat, I felt Erica would like the sweet gladvin roots. She did, and that made me happy.

Now she was curled up, sleep having taken her

quickly, tucked into my furs. I didn't mind. In fact, my feelings toward this tiny woman in my cave were far from not minding and were shifting into pleasure at her presence. She wanted to wash and learn to gather food and water. I would teach her all these things. I would prepare her for a life on this planet and hope she still chose to stay near me.

Part of me didn't trust myself around her. There were elements to my DNA, instinctual parts I could not erase that were brought to life by her scent and the softness of her skin. But I was not a beast, and I could control myself.

I was sure of it.

I was *mostly* sure of it.

Shifting the boulder in front of the cave entrance, I protected Erica from the brutal winds and frequent rains that came every night in this season. As I stoked the fire to keep it warm for her, observing the sparks as they leaped from the ground with my gentle prodding, I watched Erica sleep for a moment. I wanted her to be protected and to know she was safe with me.

When she woke, I'd had to find a way to explain to the female I needed to touch her mind so we could communicate. Then I would make her some proper clothes because the rags she had on now wouldn't do. I could teach her to forage and hunt and how to get to water she *can* reach. I shouldn't have been so amused by her attempts to get to the water when I stopped to watch her, hidden between the boulders. But I couldn't help but chuckle at the frustrated huffs of breath and the way she planted her hands on her hips, glaring at the boulder that collected rainwater as if it were to blame for her being unable to reach it.

She would be amazed by the gladvin grass, I think. It grows quickly, and the patches she and I tore up today would be replaced by the time the sun rose tomorrow. I needed to teach her how to locate the tracks of creatures she should be avoiding and how to spot those she could hunt.

There was so much of this world to show her and much to do.

If only she would let me talk to her.

I realized I was still assuming she was going to stay with me because the idea pleased me. I was designed and created for companionship, and although my brothers and I had decided it would be better if we were alone, it was difficult at times. Having a female here with her intoxicating scent and supple body was comforting.

As I watched, Erica shivered under the furs, a frown on her delicate face as her lips pouted. Was she having a bad dream? She had been through a lot, being kidnapped and taken from her home like all the others. Of course, she would still be frightened. She needed to rest and do so without being afraid.

Gently, I lay down behind her, curling my body around hers, and pulled her against me with her still bundled in the furs. She sighed and relaxed slightly against the warmth of my body, and I simply held her, creating a cradle for her with my hands and arms, and watched her sleep until sleep took me too.

ERICA

Warm and wrapped in my duvet, I sighed in contentment.

Thank God, it had all been some fucked-up dream because I was so comfortable.

Reaching out to grab my cell, I instead hit the wall.

Oops, I must be facing the wrong way.

Wait...

Keeping my eyes closed, I ran my hand across the wall next to me and traced the shapes, which almost felt like chest muscles—large and flat without nipples but definitely a chest.

When Ilk released a contented grumble, I bolted up, scampering away, and became tangled in the furs.

I had been cuddling with a goddamn alien man.

I hated that I was so warm and comfortable.

I hated that he smelled so fucking good.

And I hated that I practically swooned with the rumble that ran through his chest like a possessive purr.

But I was on an alien planet, and this was not the time to announce that I was a strong, independent woman. Because, be that as it may, I was alone and helpless, and it really seemed as though Ilk was trying to help me. He'd fed and given me water and a safe place to sleep. I could only hope his intentions were pure because I kept remembering the way he had looked at and touched me when I was exposed to him.

When I studied him, still lying in the furs although awake, he had one elbow on the floor, and his head rested in his hand, his other arm limp where I'd been asleep. I barely suppressed a squeak when I realized he had an erection, the fabric of his loincloth was not doing much to hide it. His eyes followed my gaze, and he seemed unbothered by his hardness or the fact I'd noticed. It was difficult not to look. Despite our differences, he was an impressive being. The way he kept caring for me and those hints of playfulness, it was arduous to keep my mind focused on the situation and not on the idea of him pushing me down and...

Get it together, Erica!

Less than twenty-four hours with this alien, and I was already thinking about having sex with him. There were two sides in my mind screaming conflicting thoughts at me. One was saying, *What is wrong with you, freak?* And the other was much more loudly screaming, *You're trapped on an alien planet. Fuck it! Do what you want.*

"Good morning," I said, straightening but keeping my distance.

There was a twitch of his lips like he was about to grin but stopped as he studied me. "Lurka," he grumbled out.

"Okay, you and me…" I waved my hands between us, "… need to figure out a way to communicate." He grunted and stared so intently at my hair that I subconsciously smoothed a hand over it. "Do…" I swallowed. "Do you want to touch it?" I held a lock of my hair, lifting it toward him. His green eyes locked on it, and I took a few tentative steps toward him. We had to start somewhere, I guess, and if that meant with my hair, then it would have to do. Later I could point to other items around us, and we could learn each other's words and maybe get somewhere. There was only so much we could achieve if he couldn't talk to me or I him. I wanted to explain to Ilk my situation and ask if he knew how I could get home. However small that hope was, it was still there. Just because Ilk lived in a cave didn't mean there weren't other aliens on this planet, perhaps aliens with technology that had the ability to transport me back home.

So, we had to start somewhere.

"Hair," I muttered, running my fingers through the knotted lock.

He sat up. "Herr."

"Yes, hair." As I got closer, he reached out and took the lock of hair in his fingers. I held my breath and took the final step that put me right next to him. Sitting, he was almost as tall as I was standing. "Do you think you can learn to talk to me?" I whispered. "Do you think you can help me?" My bottom lip started to tremble as the emotion threatened to overwhelm me again, as it did when I let the thoughts of where I was and how I got here take hold. "Please." I breathed the last word out. "Help me."

"Herlp," Ilk grumbled.

I gasped as he swept his other arm around my waist, pulled me onto his lap and against him, and clutched my hair in his hand, bringing it to his nose and inhaling deeply. He growled and shuddered, his arm tightening around me. *Okay, so maybe his intentions weren't so pure.* I felt the shudder of his chest under my palms as he growled, or purred, or whatever it was, a thick rumble that vibrated through me. Something nudged against my leg, and I looked down, alarmed to find his loincloth almost shifted to the side. He was still hard and *my God...*

huge. I bit back a moan. There was something so incredibly erotic about the way he inhaled as though he couldn't get enough of me.

Slowly, his fingers tangled farther into my hair, and he pressed his thumb and forefinger against my scalp.

My back stiffened. "What are you—" His eyes shifted to a milky white, and a jolt of electricity shot through my head and down my spine from his fingers. Recovering quickly, I placed my palms against his chest and shoved him. He let me go and broke the contact before I scrambled to my feet and took a handful of stumbling steps away from him.

"Sorry," he muttered.

"You should be sorry! What the fuck was that? What were you doing to m—" The words stalled in my mouth before I uttered, "Wait..." I stared at him. "Did you just speak English?"

He lifted a shoulder, then glanced at his arm with a smirk as if the gesture was as foreign to him as it was familiar to me. "Learrrn. Language." He frowned, searching for every word. "Too short. Learrrn. Small."

"Wait, wait... *wait, wait, wait.*" I started pacing the cave. "Did you learn from... touching my head?"

"A fridge." Ilk frowned, and I stared at him, not sure if to laugh or not. Okay, so maybe he really did only catch a few words. He looked at his feet, and when he raised his eyes to mine, he tried again. "Yes."

"Well, fuck me." His eyes widened, and the heavy flat part of his forehead raised like eyebrows. I held my hands up, "Figure of speech, big fella." I paced again. "So, if I let you touch my head, you can learn my language and then communicate with me?"

He paused, processing my words. "Yes."

Okay, so I had a decision to make. In order to converse with Ilk, I needed to let him do whatever he did to my brain but for longer. But what choice did I have?

Nodding, more to resolve myself than to show Ilk I agreed, I approached him once more, pausing just before I was within his arm's reach. Taking a deep breath, I took the final step and stopped next to him. Ilk snaked his fingers around my waist again, and I grabbed his wrist. His eyes found mine, and for a moment, I was lost for words, the sincerity in his expression catching me off guard. His touch was so intimate, like he was trying to comfort me and scared I would break all at once. He was the savior, and I was the injured little bird.

How can someone who looks like they're made of stone be so expressive?

"Can I sit?" I said, pointing at the floor next to him. Ilk rearranged his legs, sat cross-legged, and pulled me onto his lap. "That's not exactly what I meant. Okay, all right." His arm wrapped around me again, his hand resting on my hip. I didn't know how long this would take, or if the feeling that was like mild static shocks would turn into pain after a while, so I lifted one arm over his shoulders and pressed a palm to his chest.

Ilk looked at me, his face inches from mine, and his hand still through my hair. He held my eye contact as he pressed his fingers against my scalp again.

I must be crazy.

This was crazy.

I had no idea what the effects would be.

"Will it hurt?" I whispered, my fingers flexing on his chest. It was one thing for aliens to experiment and poke and prod me, but it was another thing entirely to *let* an alien do it. But whether it be ill-advised because I was lost or simply because he had earned it, I found I trusted Ilk.

"No pain, Errrica." His voice was deep and soothing, coupled with that rumbling growl through his chest that seemed to occur when he spoke. I felt safe and calm wrapped in his arms, but I didn't know what the long-term effects of this were or even really understood exactly what he was doing. "I take care," he rumbled out.

I nodded. Okay, so if he learned those words in the split second of contact earlier, then this shouldn't take long. "Do it."

As his fingers pressed against my scalp, his green eyes shifted to milky white again. The shock that had happened before repeated, and my fingers curled against his chest. Ilk's hand gripped my hip, and I tried to remain calm as my mind went fuzzy, his face fading in and out of focus as I struggled to keep my eyes open.

It was too much.

There was a rush of thoughts, words, numbers, and scenes. My inner monologue voice was talking through each image that passed through my mind at a breathtaking speed. But they weren't my thoughts. It was like my mind was being controlled, forced to replay not my life but my learnings. Everything I could teach Ilk was happening within seconds in a blur of colors, sensations, and sounds.

I didn't understand what I was seeing within my mind.

It was too much.

It is too mu—

CHAPTER 12

ILK

Breaking contact, I took a moment to take a handful of deep breaths. Erica's language was not so complicated, but there were a lot of sayings, slang, and gestures in addition to the words themselves. I felt her weakening, and I did not have time to get them all before I disconnected, but I had more than enough for us to be able to communicate.

Shaking my head, I looked down at Erica, slumped in my arms. She was frowning, and her pupils were darting around under her eyelids. She had lost consciousness again, but it was only for a matter of seconds this time.

I had pushed her too hard.

She was even more delicate than I had imagined.

Erica whimpered before her eyes opened, and as she focused on me, I studied the different shades of brown in her irises.

Perfection.

"Hello," she whispered.

"Hello."

"Oh my God." She sat up, clutched her head and squeezed her eyes shut before looking at me again. She was still in my lap and seemed too excited with my speech to notice. I wasn't going to remind her since I was enjoying the closeness. She was indeed as fragile as she looked, and her skin was soft beneath my hand where my fingers ran under the rags she wore. "Your pronunciation was perfect. Say my name."

"Erica."

She clapped her hands together. "This is amazing! How did you do that?"

I took a moment to work my tongue around the strange syllables of her language. "I was designed to learn and adapt. Being able to join minds to gather information makes learning more efficient. It's a skill I've developed."

"Wait! You were *designed?* Are you a robot?"

I had to search to place the word *robot*. The language would take a moment to sync with me, and soon I wouldn't need to search for the words. "No. I'm a synthetic organism. I am alive."

"Who made you?"

"My history is not important right now. That's a conversation for another time."

She smirked. "Just learned my language and already shutting me down. Ouch."

Erica was joking with me, and it was cute. Simply my learning her language had relaxed her, and she was different than she was before. I enjoyed playing these word games with her. While I didn't quite understand the context of her jest, it didn't matter. I smiled, and her smirk widened into a grin.

After a beat, her smile dropped, and her voice became quieter. "Can you help me?" The tone of her plea pulled at my chest. I wanted to help her more than anything, but I didn't know if I could offer her the kind of assistance she wanted.

"I will help you, Erica. I will make you new clothes and show you how to gather food and water. You are welcome to stay here with me, or I can teach you how to build a shelter..." She nodded as my words trailed off, her soft lips turned down. I sighed. "You miss your home."

Erica jerked away from me when I lifted a finger to wipe away a tear before she relaxed again and let me brush her cheek. The ache returned to my chest at the lingering fear still within her. She trusted me because she had no choice, but if she could find a way home to her own planet, she would go. I witnessed a world of emotions play across her face, and her small hand sprawled out on my chest.

"I can't go back, can I?" she whispered.

I couldn't lie to her. "I'm sorry, Erica. No."

A few more tears escaped, and instead of brushing them away, I pulled her against me. She resisted for only a second before resting her head on my shoulder and her palms on my chest as she cried.

I hurt with her.

It was difficult to explain to Erica, but I understood her pain. My pain was of a different sort, but it was still pain. I had left my home because the Ghaal had dark souls and hearts. Many of the Ghaal had already fled the planet, certain the answer to their problems lay in another solar system where breeding could be expedited and their fertility issues combatted. This happened long before Synths were designed to help bring back their species from the brink of extinction. When we came to be, there was only one remaining colony, nature having taken over the remnants of cities and civilizations elsewhere. But the Ghaal who remained created us, synthetic organic life forms designed to adapt. It was the last experiment of a dying scientist, his knowledge dying with him.

The idea was brilliant. We could adapt to the environment and change our bodies for whatever was required, including gender so we could breed. We were able to make ourselves fertile, make children designed to adapt, and we could save the Ghaal. We could survive any planet or terrain, and were bred with a libido to match the genetic perfection of our bodies. We could eat and drink almost anything without repercussions and no longer needed to be concerned about the scarcity of food that was only in the past few decades starting to repair. Chemical warfare had destroyed not only their species but many others as well. The planet was still healing.

The Synths were to be the answer to bringing back the Ghaal species from the brink of extinction.

Until we weren't.

With an increased ability to adapt our bodies came the advanced ability to learn and enhanced intelligence.

As well as enhanced empathy.

My brothers and I recognized the Ghaal for what they were—a violent and selfish species which thrived on war and slavery, and this had caused them to almost wipe out themselves.

They were *not* worth saving.

Erica's sadness affected me. I knew what it was like to leave your home behind and be separated from your family. It's different, though—my choice wasn't easy, but it was still a *choice.* Erica was taken from her home against her will and dumped galaxies away.

I don't blame her for crying for hours this morning until her beautiful brown eyes were rimmed red and her pale skin blotched with an angry pink. She stayed on my lap, curled up against me, and cried until she fell into an exhausted sleep and took a short nap while still in my arms.

I hurt with her.

My heart ached with her.

Erica watched me now as I was preparing to make her new clothing. The thin rags she wore would be destroyed quickly, snag on every branch, and do nothing to protect her from the winds every night. She had washed her face and taken a grateful gulp of water after waking and was now lifting and feeling different types of furs, checking for allergies and comfort.

"Which are your most vulnerable parts?" I asked.

Erica looked at me from the other side of the cave. Her mouth fell open as she stuttered through an answer, but all she eventually said was, "Pardon?"

"Your most vulnerable parts," I repeated. I didn't understand her hesitation. It made sense to cover the parts of her that were most delicate. While I looked at her and decided she was *all* delicate, I couldn't dress her head to toe in furs and keep her hidden in my cave, though I liked that idea. When she still looked at me, I held the furs I was going to sew together in front of my body. "I cover my feet," I said, indicating my boots, "… and my genitals."

Erica coughed, and it turned into a splutter as her eyes fell to my where my aching cock lay under my loincloth. Her cheeks flamed pink, and she looked away. I smiled, watching her reaction. This was a different pink on her cheeks than from when she cried earlier. I searched for the reaction in my mind. "Does talking about your body embarrass you?"

"No! Well… I mean… not usually. But you're practically a stranger."

"Do you need help deciding?"

"No. I… I… what do you mean?" She continued to stutter as I approached her, growing ever aware of how small she was the closer I got. When she stood at full height, she was facing my stomach, and as I drew up next to her, she craned her neck up to hold my eye contact. Her cheeks were still pink, but she didn't look away.

I crouched in front of her, and although I knew it was a mistake to touch her, I couldn't help myself. She had been with me for less than a day, and I had to keep reminding myself not to push her too far. But Erica's scent intoxicated me, and when she was before me like this, her small chest heaving with quickened breaths, I lost a little bit more of the control I was barely holding onto.

I traced my fingers down her arms. "Do these need protection?"

"Sometimes," she breathed out the word, shuddering, although it wasn't cold. "Your sun is very bright, and I may get sunburned."

"Being burned by your own planet's sun? That is strange," I said absentmindedly, lifting my hands from her arms and placing them on her legs. "How about here?"

"Um… yes. If we're going to be walking through a forest or anything."

She lifted her foot delicately when I ran my hands down her legs. "Here?"

She cleared her throat. "Yes, please. I need shoes."

I hummed, too distracted by the feel of her skin under my hands to say much. She was so incredibly soft, and although I had only touched her a handful of times, every time, it floored me.

How did she survive being so soft? I would have to ask more about her planet.

When I lifted my head, she was staring at me, not moving nor telling me to stop. I didn't want to push it too far and frighten her again, but it was difficult to resist touching her more. My pheromones lifted, and her eyelids went heavy. I inhaled again, desperate to get more of her intoxicating scent. She wanted to bathe, she had told me this morning after she had washed her face, and I would take her to a place where she could. But even as she was, her scent drew me in. My chest rumbled with a barely contained growl, my instincts awakening every second she was close. Her eyes flashed with lust, and my gaze traveled up to the mounds of her breasts, her nipples tightening under the thin fabric of her rags. Her useless clothing was so thin I could see the outline of her breasts, round and perfect. I caught her eye again, and she knew I had been looking.

But still, she didn't stop me.

Gently, slowly, so slowly so as to make sure she felt safe, I traced my hands up her body. Her rags lifted as I raised my hands from her thighs to her torso, exposing her stomach, and she trembled as my breath met her belly. I ran my hands up farther and cupped her breasts. Internally, there was a steady stream of thoughts in my mind telling me to stop, but it was too late. Her breasts rested so perfectly in my palms, completely encompassed by the size of my hands. She gasped at the contact, then sighed, my thumbs grazing the underside of her breasts, skin on skin as her rags had lifted farther.

My breathing had become ragged, every touch of her sparking the part of me I had long thought I had better control over. Deep down, I was an animal, and no amount of intelligence would cover that if I were to get her under me. If she were to let me inside her, that part of me would take over.

And still, she didn't tell me to stop.

"And here," I whispered, the words coming out as a low growl. "Do you need protection here?"

"Yes." Her voice was small, barely a whisper in the air, and when she shifted against me, I growled again.

"Erica," I breathed out. "I don't wish to do anything that makes you uncomfor—"

"It's okay." She rushed the words, then took a steadying breath. "Um... just touching is okay. Just... touching." She cleared her throat. "For the clothes, right?"

I couldn't help it and leaned forward as I hummed my agreement and placed my mouth on her exposed stomach. I needed to taste and experience her. She gasped, her hands balling into fists at her sides, but she didn't tell me to stop. I massaged her breasts and flicked my tongue across the skin of her stomach, dipping into her belly button. I didn't have a belly button, and hers was so delicate like the rest of her.

She made a slight squeaking sound as my tongue reached the edge of her rags, and I stopped, groaning loudly and pulling away from her.

She had made that sound before when she was afraid, and I wouldn't do anything to frighten her.

Erica fidgeted, pulling her top down, her cheeks

still flamed pink as she looked away from me.

"I'm sorry," I said, stood, grabbed the furs I had long forgotten and moved to the other side of the cave to begin making her clothing. "I won't harm you."

"I know," she squeaked out, glancing everywhere but at me.

I looked down at my lap, ready to busy myself with my work.

Erica *must* feel safe here.

Because whether I was ready to admit it or not, I already knew I wanted her to stay with me.

Erica would leave me if she felt unsafe, and I didn't think I could go back to being alone without her.

CHAPTER 13

ERICA

Holy. Shit.

One night.

One fucking night.

And I had already let Ilk manhandle me. *Or... alienhandle.*

I couldn't explain it.

I felt *safe* with him.

My entire life had been turned upside down, and I'd landed on the doorstep of someone who, or so it appeared, only wanted to look after me. It's not even that I'd ever felt particularly unsafe on Earth, but I'd also never been held the way Ilk held or touched me with such gentleness as if I was the most spectacular thing he'd ever seen. The way his gaze took me in, as if I was too magnificent to behold, was empowering. I knew he wouldn't hurt me, and when his huge hands wandered my body, he kept looking up at me, waiting for me to tell him to stop, and he would have too. The second I told him no, he would have removed his hands and moved away. I knew that with every fiber of my being.

So why didn't I tell him to stop?

Because I shouldn't be finding a big stone-looking alien man attractive, and I definitely shouldn't feel the flush of warmth between my legs at his touch. I wanted to touch him back, but I was scared to pull on that thread, afraid I might not be able to stop myself. If I stood there with my arms at my sides and let him suck and kiss at my skin and massage my tits, then I could tell myself I wasn't taking an active part and maintaining some sanity. Even though, under his touch, I gnawed on my lip and bit back the moan that threatened to escape the moment his hot mouth met my skin.

Was I *that* starved for affection I'd do it with an alien?

Watching his large arms flex and shift as he worked, his hands moved so delicately across the hide he was sewing into clothes for me, I realized, *Yes, yes, I damn well would.*

Because why not, right? I couldn't get home. I was

literally galaxies away with no one here to judge me but myself and Ilk, I guess, but the way he looked at me told me there would be no judgment. I hadn't wanted to cry in front of him earlier, afraid I might in some way offend him or make him think I wasn't grateful for all he was doing because I was, *so* much, but I couldn't hold it in. Everything was too overwhelming, and whenever I stopped for more than a second to think about it too much, it would overcome me again.

I kept thinking of the other girls. Had they found stone aliens to look after them too? Or were they wandering the woods, unsure of what to eat and drink? Or being chased by some creatures the likes of which I couldn't even imagine?

I shuddered, and the movement drew Ilk's gaze. So I gave him a hesitant smile, and he returned it with that big goofy grin of his, the awkwardness of him pulling away from me moments before apparently forgotten. I relaxed a bit and watched him work because standing here perving on an alien was much better for the soul than sinking into despair about something which I could do nothing about.

If I wanted to look for the girls, would Ilk help me?

I was starting to feel useless and like I was taking advantage of him while he sat there and handmade me some new clothes, with thread made from God knows what and a large bone needle. If I were going to ask the mammoth favor of having Ilk trek across his planet for the other girls, I needed to help him back and show I was at least making an effort.

"Is there..." my voice was small, and I cleared my throat and spoke up. "Is there anything I can do to help?"

"I don't think so, Erica. When I have finished this, we will go fetch some food."

"I can do it." His hands stalled in their sewing, and he gazed up at me from under his heavy, flat brow. "I mean... if you tell me where to go, is there something I can get for us?"

His fingers were twitching, and he appeared to be thinking it over, his gaze sweeping up and down my body. His lips twitched. "Do you remember the gladvin field from yesterday?"

"Gladvin?"

"The grass with the tasty roots."

"Oh, yes! I can get those."

Ilk chuckled. "We cannot survive only on roots. We need something with more sustenance. But I don't think you're ready to hunt." He was smirking again, and I folded my arms across my chest. I know I was a stranger here, but he didn't need to constantly smirk at my efforts. Then I remembered the water bag he had left for me yesterday—he knew I needed it and couldn't reach the water on top of the boulder. Was he watching and laughing at me then too? My cheeks flushed again, and I waited. "Slightly beyond that field are the moobark trees."

"The tall thin ones? White?"

"Yes. You can strip the bark off them. It's not as sweet as the gladvin roots but much more nutritious. Would you like to gather some for us?"

He emphasized the word *us,* and a tingle ran down my spine. I straightened. "Yep, I can do that. Back soon." I practically skipped to the opening of the cave before stopping, my fingers tapping on the edge as I hovered on the precipice before leaving. "Ilk?"

"Yes, Erica?"

I liked how he said my name, and I resisted the urge to twirl my hair around my finger. "Is uh... there any creatures or anything out there I should be aware of?"

He looked at me for a long moment before he answered, bordering on an uncomfortable pause, "Not near here, no. This area is fairly clear of wildlife."

I wanted to ask him why. Or maybe I didn't. So I simply nodded.

Ilk was still smirking at me as I turned and left the cave, slipping through the gap he had created by shoving the boulder to the side that he pushed in front of the entrance overnight. I was fairly confident I remembered where the grass was and located it quite quickly. Stopping to investigate, I found the patches I had ripped out yesterday had already grown back. Good to know it was so quick to replenish. Looking up, I spotted the nearest patch of trees and moved toward them, cautious of every nearby sound. I saw no animals as Ilk promised and wondered if perhaps more lived in the areas that were less rocky with additional food. Apart from Ilk and whatever little bird things lived in the trees, there didn't seem to be much life around these rocks. I'd have to ask him why later when I was feeling bolder.

Reaching the trees, I picked at the bark. While it looked feathery, it certainly didn't feel that soft but more like rubber. I pulled a face, unsure what it would feel like to eat strips of rubber, but *when in Rome,* I guess. Finding the edge of a piece, I grabbed it between two fingers and pulled. This resulted only in my fingers slipping from the bark.

Okay, so it's tougher than it looks.

I picked at it with my fingernails until there was enough to grab on to and yanked down. But it still didn't budge, and with all the weight I put on it, the strip came away from the tree only an inch.

"Yep, no problem, Ilk. Just pull the bark off the damn tree because it's that simple when we're not made of stone," I mumbled to myself, getting frustrated when I tried another piece of bark and then another tree, still unable to make the strips peel away. So far, my mission to show Ilk that I could be helpful—and not simply a burden he needed to look after—was not going well. I continued trying to no avail and lost track of how long I was out there, endeavoring to pull bark from a damn tree. How fucking hard could it be? But no matter which angle I tried, how hard I gripped, or the leverage I attempted by planting my foot against the trunk, the damn thing simply... Would. *Not.* Budge.

In my frustration, I grabbed the trunk with both hands and shook the tree, shouting at it for being so difficult. A flock of the small creatures I had seen earlier fled, flying in all directions and disappearing into other foliage. "Sorry," I muttered. Still not satiated, I decided to shake the tree a few more times. "Stupid. Fucking. *Tree!*"

Spinning on my heel when there was a deep chuckle behind me, I found Ilk standing a few feet back. I had no idea how long he had been there watching me struggle. Apparently, he could move around silently if he wanted to. *Good to know.*

"Your clothes are ready, Erica," he said, a twinkle of mischief in his eyes. "Are you having trouble with the bark?"

"You set me up! You knew it would be too hard for me to get." He simply smiled that lopsided grin at me, and I lost my patience. I knew I was being rash, but I was faced with trying to find a place for myself on a strange planet, and at every moment and at every turn, I was being shown that I didn't fit in. The emotions were boiling up inside me, and I didn't need an alien man laughing at my attempts to top it off. I sighed loudly. "Oh, go fuck yourself, Ilk."

His smile dropped, and the second the words were from my lips, I felt guilty. I held out a hand and was about to apologize when he turned and walked back toward his cave. "Dammit, *dammit, DAMMIT!*" I shook the tree a dozen more times, now feeling useless, angry, lost, *and* guilty. Waiting a few moments longer, I cursed a few more times before going after Ilk.

He moved fast and was nowhere to be seen, and I assumed he had already made it back to the cave. So, I had failed to show I could be helpful and now offended the only alien who hadn't tried to poke me with weird, cold instruments. *Fuck.*

When I made it back to the cave, I was out of breath, having hoofed it over the rocky area to get back quicker. Ilk was standing toward the rear wall of the cave, half hidden in shadow with his back to me.

"Ilk, I—"

He turned around, and I froze.

My gaze dropped to his crotch. He had pulled aside his loincloth and had his cock in his hand, pumping vigorously. I stuttered a handful of times, unable to form any words. His cock was a fucking monster, and I guess I should have known, looking at the size and build of Ilk. Like him, it was a stone purple-gray, but unlike the rest of him, it wasn't smooth, instead covered in small bumps and ridges up to the bulbous head that was currently dripping with clear precum. Ilk held my gaze when I finally forced my focus from his hand, working his cock up and down, seemingly completely unabashed at being caught.

"Ilk... I... I..." Fuck. I had no words. His eyelids were lowered, his gaze heavy with lust as he watched me watch him touch himself.

"I don't yet understand all the nuances of your language," he said, his voice gravelly with pleasure as he hummed. "You told me to go fuck myself..." He approached me, and I stood frozen on the spot. "Did I misunderstand? Was I supposed to wait for you to join me?" He was right next to me now, his vigorous strokes having slowed to a leisurely pace. His cock was near my chest, and I had the sudden urge to taste it. "Were you meant to witness me fucking myself?"

I wanted to tell him I was sorry and that he misunderstood. However, I was glad I hadn't offended him, but as he held my eye contact, his green eyes blazing with lust, I simply couldn't find the words. Ilk lifted his other hand and touched my face, drawing his hand away sharply when I flinched and paused before stroking my cheek again. "Errrica," he purred my name out like he did when we first met, drawing out the 'r' in a sexy growl, and when I only whimpered in response, he hummed, the deep rumble working through his chest. "You bring out a side of me I haven't known in a long time."

This information didn't help me gather my thoughts. I just nodded, my eyes dropping again to where he worked himself. I couldn't help it—it was sexy as fuck the way he touched himself without embarrassment or worry. We were alone in this intimate space, and suddenly I was all too aware of the clothes on my body. I rubbed my thighs together, desperate for contact. Should I touch myself too? Would he think me strange or easy if we got ourselves off together? It's all I could think about with him standing in front of me like this, and I needed to deal with these desires to think straight.

At least, that's the flimsy excuse I gave myself.

I touched my hands to my stomach, and Ilk followed the movement with his gaze. When I dipped my hand into the waistband of my shorts, he groaned, licking his lips.

I would explain to him what *go fuck yourself* meant later because right now, my mind must not be right. I felt light-headed and was simply aching with need for release. I felt if I didn't do something about this right now, I would forget how to breathe while the need overtook me.

Sinking to the cave floor, I leaned against the cool

wall and slid my shorts and underwear down, kicking them both off. They still had a hole over my crotch, but I didn't want to be reminded of that right now, instead deciding I might as well get lost in this moment. Another rumble worked its way through Ilk's massive chest as I spread my legs, running my fingers between my pussy lips and moaning for him.

He kneeled in front of me, and I stiffened, but he didn't touch me, his eyes fixated on my pussy as I pressed a fingertip to my clit and worked it in small circles. God, I was so turned on. I kept my eyes on his cock, imagining what it might feel like to try to take that monster inside me. I imagined Ilk would be gentle, but he'd also fuck me senseless if I asked him to.

That last thought sent a tremble down my spine and a rush through my pussy. My legs twitched as I felt my orgasm building, and Ilk was breathing deeply as though he could smell my arousal, his hand working double-time around his cock. I eyed his fingers. They weren't small, one perhaps the thickness of three of mine.

His fingers had me transfixed, and I remembered how he had touched me before.

Oh my God, I was really going to do this.

"Ilk," I whispered and gasped when he looked at me, his expression animal. I swallowed, wanting so badly to ask but so fucking nervous. "Would you please… put a finger inside my pussy?"

He moaned loudly, and I jumped a bit as the sound reverberated throughout the cave. I glanced around as though expecting someone to pop out, having heard the sound. But we were alone, we were safe, and I was too turned on to care anyway.

Still pumping his cock, he moved forward, bending at the hips and holding his index finger out, sweeping it once between my pussy lips and growling when I moaned.

"Please…" I begged him, pushing aside the thought that I was *begging a fucking alien to finger fuck me.* "I'm so close." Hesitation gone, Ilk pressed his finger into my waiting pussy, stretching me around him. "Oh *fuck!*" I cried out, opening my legs wider. I couldn't last, not as he started pumping his finger in and out in time with him working his cock. I came hard around his finger, crying out and shuddering around him, continuing to touch my clit until I was completely spent.

Ilk's peak followed shortly after, spraying his clear cum across the cave floor.

As I lay against the cave wall, panting and limp, a familiar sense of shame started to creep over me. I may claim to be a *strong, independent woman,* but sexually liberated I was not. It was too ingrained in me from social expectations to culture, that I wasn't comfortable being as open about sex and play as Ilk apparently was. Ilk removed his finger from me, dipping it into his mouth and sucking it clean, his eyes closing in the ecstasy of my taste. I shuddered, the shame shoved from my mind watching him. It was fucking hot, but the lust was mixing with the realization I had just had a mutual masturbation session with an alien, and my thoughts were going haywire.

Humans were not equipped to deal with this shit.

I opened my mouth to apologize to Ilk, maybe about the misunderstanding that led to this, or perhaps because I now felt I had led him on, but before I could get a word out, Ilk leaned forward farther and pressed his tongue against my pussy, taking one slow lick from my ass all the way up and over my clit. He did it again, and I gripped the thin fabric of my top, unsure if I should push him away or not.

I should stop him.

I *really* should.

But then he ran his tongue, flat and heavy, over my clit again, vibrations running through me as he rumbled with a satisfied hum.

I should stop him.

Really. I should.

Oh!

Fuuuck...

CHAPTER 14

ILK

She tasted heavenly, my Erica.

I know it was wrong to think of her as mine and that I should be teaching her only to survive, perhaps encouraging her to go find the others who dropped in the units with her, with me tailing along at a distance, just enough to keep her safe. But the second I smelled her arousal and tasted her on my skin, she was *mine*. Erica had already come with me, and the sounds she made as she shuddered and her cunt clenched around my finger were too much.

I simply had to taste more of her.

She squealed with delight as I gripped her hips and dragged her forward, shuffling back myself so she could lie down while I ravished her. Erica reached forward and grabbed the back of my head, pulling me closer between her legs as she spread them wider for me. She had touched that little nub above the entrance to her cunt to make herself come, so I focused on that, running my tongue over and around it.

"Suck on it… please suck on my clit."

Erica's begging was so sweet, and who was I to refuse? I promised myself I would take care of her, look after and keep her safe. And right now, I was taking care of Erica in the best possible way, bringing her pleasure and forcing another orgasm from her so soon after her previous one. She would know then, even more than before, that I could take care of and keep her happy as well as safe.

Did she have someone on her home planet who could please her as I did? A growl rumbled through my throat at the thought and awakened the animal part of me. I focused on the sounds that fell deliciously from her lips to calm myself and instead felt my cock harden again. I gyrated against the cave floor, desperate for friction.

Pursing my lips, I worried that my skin was too rough against hers, so soft and delicate. But as I sucked on the little nub she liked so much, she cried out, gripped my head with her nails, and held me in place. Lifting my hand, I pressed my finger against her entrance, waiting for a protest I hoped wouldn't come. When she didn't tell me to stop, I pressed it inside, and her cries of ecstasy hit a new pitch. I'd never heard sounds like that before. Her incoherent mumbling and cries as she bucked against me were the only sounds I wanted to hear from now on.

Pumping my finger in and out of her slick cunt, I felt her peak coming as she tightened around me and continued my assault on her clit. With a rush of warmth, she came, and I kept sucking, relishing in the way she cried out louder with each suck.

"Stop, stop, Ilk. Please stop. It's too much."

Reluctantly, I pulled away, and her arms dropped to her sides, her legs hung open, and her chest heaved as she closed her eyes. Erica looked so breathtakingly beautiful. The rags she still wore had slipped up when I dragged her toward me, and her breasts were exposed to me, small pink nipples pointed with her arousal. Considering her earlier embarrassment, she seemed unconcerned with her almost full nudity, and I was pleased she was becoming more comfortable around me. I watched her cunt, twitching with every jolt of her leg in her post-orgasmic bliss, and growled low as I imagined sinking my cock into her cunt. She was so tight around my fingers that I would have to make sure she was wet and ready before I tried to penetrate her. But I would have her making those delicious cries of pleasure again with my cock, of that I was sure.

After a while, she drew her legs together, pulling the rags down to cover her breasts. I grumbled at this, and she looked up at me at the sound. Erica cleared her throat, and I smiled at her. She was uncomfortable again. Apparently, her nudity did embarrass her—another cultural thing I must ask her about. I envisioned long nights of making her moan, followed by long conversations where she tells me about her planet, and I tell her about mine.

"So, um…" Erica cleared her throat again, "… you said my clothes were ready."

"Yes." I adjusted my loincloth, watching Erica's eyes seek the movement. "Come, you can try them on." As she stood, she moved to pull her rags back over her legs. I held my hand out, stilling her movement. "You do not need to put those back on."

"But I can't just walk around with half a shirt on."

I chuckled, eyeing her bare ass as she turned to search for her new clothes. "You can walk around without any clothes on if you like."

She threw a hand on her hip and tilted it, offering me a smirk. "You'd never be able to concentrate."

"All I'd need to concentrate on are the sounds you make when you come." I let a low growl accompany my words and smiled at the way she pressed her thighs together.

"Um…" She ran a hand through her hair, her fingers getting tangled in the knots. Her eyes darted around for a moment longer before resting on mine, and when they did, she held my gaze. When she spoke again, her voice was nothing more than a breathy whisper, "Please stop looking at me like that."

"Like what?"

"Like you want to..." Erica's voice trailed off, and a quick succession of expressions played across her face. She bit her lip and almost smiled at me, but then her brow furrowed, and her cheeks flushed pink. I swelled with pride, knowing she was attracted to me, and ached to know the feeling of my cock penetrating her tight cunt. But she was also shy and new to this planet, with a lot to learn. Erica still held fear inside her, and I would not rush her.

A hum rumbled through my throat, and I bent to retrieve the clothes I had made her, beckoning her over to me. She cupped her hands in front of the hair that covered her mound and rushed toward me with small steps. I bent on one knee in front of her and held the pants, ready for her to step into. When she lifted a leg to put them on, I was hit with another rush of her scent and growled again. She froze, and I chuckled.

"No need to fear me, Erica. You just smell so good, I want to—"

"I know what you want to do." Erica rushed out the words, and I chuckled again. Where had this part of me been all these years? Had I lost more than my libido and mating instinct when I separated from my brothers? I don't recall being anything more than a stoic being, doing my duty to protect the innocent from the Ghaal and keeping my distance. Hunting, feeding, and sleeping, and I was nothing more. But there were parts of me returning now—I was laughing and playing, and it was all thanks to Erica.

With every passing hour, I wanted to keep her closer, like she was a part of me I had lost. I couldn't imagine going back to how it was before her.

Erica stepped into the pants, and I pulled them up, cinching them around her waist with a cord. I'd made them a bit large, forgetting just how small she was, but I could adjust them another time. Once she had slipped on the boots and the cloak, she appeared dwarfed by the furs. Erica looked down, holding her arms out and swaying back and forth.

"Are they suitable?"

She smiled at me. "They're kinda cute. I never knew teal was my color." As I moved to stand, she placed her hand on my head, and I stilled, holding back a hum of contentment as she absentmindedly stroked her thumb across my forehead. "One thing, though…" she said. "Is there something I can wrap around my… chest?"

I searched the floor for a scrap of fur, holding one up. She nodded, and I shrugged. "Lift your cloak."

She held the edges of the flowing garment and watched me before slowly lifting it so I had a view of her beautiful breasts. Her little nipples puckered again when my breath was close, but I strained to resist the urge to touch them. I wrapped the cloth around under her armpits, and Erica giggled.

"No, no, not like that. I need it to cover my boobs."

"Why would you want to do that?"

She gestured, and I held the cloak edges as she wrapped the strip over her breasts, pulling it around her back and tying it in a simple knot under her breasts. "Because it's nice to have support." She held her breasts and jiggled them slightly, stopping when she realized what she was doing and saw the look on my face, slack-jawed and entranced by their movement. Erica barely suppressed her laughter and laughed harder when she had to coax me to release the cloak when all I wanted to do was stare at her body. "Stop staring at me, you perve."

"Perve?" I stood.

"I thought you learned my language?"

"I learned the words but didn't have enough time to pick up on slang words and nuances."

"Ah... that explains the *go-fuck-yourself* incident," she said.

"Incident? Didn't you enjoy yourself?"

"I did." Erica's cheeks flushed again, and I grinned with pride. "But when someone says that, it's not meant to be taken literally. It can be an insult..." When my smile dropped, she held up her hands, stepping toward me and placing them on my chest. "No, no. Please, let me finish… I didn't mean to insult you. I was angry and feeling useless and lost, and I got irritated when I couldn't get the damn bark off the tree. I snapped at you out of emotion, and I shouldn't have, so I'm sorry."

She squealed as I leaned down and buried my face against her neck, inhaling sharply as she giggled, lightly slapping at my shoulders. "If you really feel you owe me an apology, I know how you can do it."

"Oh God, *Ilk…*"

The way she said my name stirred my instincts further. *Who was this Synth I was becoming?* Flirting with a female, and every time she reciprocated, giving away her desires with a look or a slight touch, the hold I had on myself severed a little more. I was never a savage being, but this was something else. This was something I had never experienced, not even when I resided with the Ghaal. They never made me feel like this because, to them, I was an experiment, nothing more than a means to an end, and although I was intelligent and empathetic, they never saw us as equals. But to Erica, I am her savior, her protector, her only friend on this planet, and I have a reason to live and not only survive.

Her hands were still on my chest, and she giggled again as I nibbled at her neck. "Ilk, Ilk, please. You promised you'd show me where to bathe, and I'm hungry too."

I pulled my lips from her neck and took in her flushed cheeks. So perfect. Straightening, I left only one hand on the small of her back, content she'd allowed me to continue touching her. "You're right. Come with me and bring your water bag."

She adjusted her cloak and beamed up at me.

Looking at her, I felt more alive than I had in many years.

CHAPTER 15

ERICA

There were two ways of looking at this situation, I thought, but I'd continue that thought later as I was momentarily distracted by the impressive spring Ilk had taken me to. The water was warmer than the cool air, made harsher by brisk winds that seemed to pick up as the day went on. Tiny swirls of steam hovered around the surface of the springs, consisting of dozens of small holes in and around the base of the mountain, some big enough for just me, some big enough for four of Ilk. The one I stood next to now was the size of a small spa, a crevice in the rocks, one of many other springs dotted around an area slightly higher up the mountains than Ilk's cave. It had taken us about an hour or so to walk here, and I'm certain it would have been quicker if I'd been able to move across the rock formations with the same skill as Ilk had. He'd offered to carry me, but I was determined to maintain some level of independence.

If I were to call this planet home, I needed to be able to look after myself whether I stayed with Ilk or not.

I really wanted to stay with him because why would I go adventuring into the unknown when I had a comfortable and warm place to stay, was fed and watered, and now had the ability to bathe? Not to mention the sexy gargoyle-esque alien who seemed intent on keeping me safe and pleasing me.

In more ways than one.

I looked out over the horizon. We were higher than I had originally thought, and I could see the weird gray ocean. Geography wasn't a subject I was ever particularly good at in school, so I had no idea how the moon, which appeared larger and brighter than the one back home, the outline of it visible even in the daytime, affected the tides.

It was a breathtaking sight but also terrifying. I think one of the pods had headed toward the ocean, and I hoped she was okay.

Back near Ilk's cave, from the entrance, I could see the blurry outline of the forest in the distance, and I was *certain* another pod had landed near there. I placed a hand on my chest as my heart thrummed against my ribs, creating an ache when I thought of the other girls. It struck me how quickly I had accepted this was my new home because this was the dream, right? Living off the land, no bills, no large cities, no distractions, just you, the earth, and those you chose to be with.

But no matter how comfortable I could be here, I needed to find the other girls. I'm sure they would do the same for me. Although we were practically strangers, few things in life bonded you closer than a weird-ass alien abduction, and I hated the idea they were wandering around lost, searching for each other and me when I was here about to have a bath.

I would need to talk to Ilk about finding them.

My attention was drawn back to the bath as a large bubble formed on the surface and then popped.

"How is the water so warm?" I asked Ilk.

"Lava," he rumbled.

"Lava... wait... as in this mountain is a volcano?"

Ilk chuckled, presumably at the panic in my voice. "It's not dangerous. There are several spots on the other side of the mountain where the lava and pressure are released."

I watched the water bubble and steam for a moment as I considered this, and my hand shot to my throat as I choked out a horrified sound. Ilk looked up in alarm, and I glanced at him, tears forming in my eyes. "One of the other girls went over that side of the mountain, I'm sure of it. What if she landed in a pothole of lava and was burned alive?"

Ilk's expression softened. "The units wouldn't fit in the craters. She may have been bounced around, but she would not have been burned alive." He stared at me for a moment longer as I unsuccessfully tried to wipe my expression clear. "I assure you she is safe."

Desperation crawled at my skin to begin the journey to look for them, but I was also covered in days and days of filth, and washing with a rag and a water bag simply wasn't cutting it anymore. The idea my selfishness may be putting the others in danger plucked at my chest, and I swallowed back the urge to cry. *Please, please, just let me have a bath, and then I will ask Ilk about finding them.*

I took a long, leveling breath and tried to calm myself. Ilk was still watching me with concern. It seemed he was intent on looking after me, and when I had tried to do something as simple as skip the morning meal, he wouldn't let up.

Bath first, then rescue.

Bath first, then rescue.

Lord, please forgive me for this act of selfishness.

Speaking of acts of selfishness, I eyed Ilk, smiling, so he relaxed and continued filling the water bags he had brought with him from the tops of boulders I couldn't hope to reach. His muscles flexed as he reached up, and that brought my thoughts back to the two potential viewpoints on this whole bath situation.

Either getting naked around Ilk was a really bad idea because, as the hours had gone on, he had become increasingly flirty and touchy, and while I was loving it—although I wouldn't admit that bit yet—I'm not sure I was ready for sex with his hulking alien form.

On the other hand, maybe getting naked around Ilk was a fucking fantastic idea because something about being around him was erotic, and I was becoming more turned on every minute. The steam from the hot springs must be making me dizzy, as when I eyed him through the haze and inhaled deeply, that masculine scent that lingered around him strengthened. It was impossible to look at him and not think of sex. *Did that make me even more selfish?* Perhaps. It had been too long since I'd been with someone, and some two-pump-chump one-night stands weren't doing it for me. *Was I taking advantage of Ilk? Using him for my pleasure?* Maybe, and I felt a twinge of guilt at that. I didn't know how his culture worked. Maybe sex was a non-verbal lifetime commitment or something, but it's not like I'd be the only one to get off.

Ilk had already shown himself capable of

pleasing me with his mouth and fingers, and a big part of me was aching to know what it felt like to have his cock inside me.

I continued to watch him, and if I shook my head, the haze from the steam would clear slightly, but *he* was still appealing to me. I hated to admit it, and I wouldn't verbalize it, but I think I had already decided what I wanted to do to this gorgeous creature in front of me.

Or, more specifically, what I wanted *him* to do to *me*.

Ilk turned as I stood at the edge of the spring, frowning slightly and glancing between the water and me before smiling. "Is this all right?" he asked. His smile crept into a look of sheer pride, a slightly smug grin adorning his large face, and I smirked. He already knew the answer. He was fishing for compliments.

"This is perfect," I said, dipping my toe into the water, having already removed my boots and humming at the pleasant temperature. "I don't suppose you have soap?"

He paused for a moment, frowning, then smiling again. "The gladvin roots would do what you are seeking." He paused, his eyes watching where I stood near the surface of the water. "You wish to be clean."

"The gladvin roots? But don't we eat those?"

Ilk grinned again. "As a treat, yes. They are

refreshing but have little nutritional value. If you squeeze out the juice, you can use it to clean."

"Okay, I'll go grab some."

"Stay here and get in the water. I'll get them."

I nodded and pulled my cloak over my head. Ilk eyed the strap of fabric I had used to cover my breasts and scowled but returned my smirk when he met my eyes before setting off. No doubt he remembered how slowly I had moved through the mountains. He would move faster without me.

The second he was out of sight, I wanted to shout after him—the bubbling of the water suddenly sounded menacing instead of comforting. The entire idea of being on an alien planet was scary enough without being alone. But surely, he wouldn't leave me here by myself if I were in danger? This area, much like the grassy field around his cave, appeared to be devoid of life. Was it just Ilk here alone? *Was* he *the reason there wasn't much wildlife around?* Perhaps they were afraid of him.

Or an even more troubling thought, *Was there something else here that all the animals wanted to avoid?*

Shivering and not entirely from the chill of the wind, I hurried to undo the fabric from around my chest and pull my new pants off. Folding them, I laid them carefully on the ground within reach of the spring and slid into the warm water. I was thankful

Ilk wasn't around to hear the way I moaned when I was submerged up to my neck—it felt like heaven. I was always more of a shower than a bath person, but after being captive and then having to relieve myself in a field, being able to clean myself was nothing short of ecstasy.

The spring was crystal clear, and there would be no covering my body from Ilk, but the water felt too good for me to care. I paddled around the spring, and soon Ilk returned, bending to offer me a handful of roots. I tilted backward to dunk my head and wet my hair before squeezing one of the root berries into my palm and then over my hair. It didn't lather at all and felt more like a slightly oily serum, but it was better than nothing, so I worked it through my hair and over my body as best I could.

My hair was another issue. It was thick and wavy and never cooperated. Usually, I would straighten it, but that was no longer an option, and it was now a bundle of knots. The oil from the roots helped work out some of them, but it wouldn't do for much longer.

Maybe it would be easier to chop it off. But for now, I'd ask for a strip of leather and tie it up and out of the way.

The water sloshed against my back as Ilk sank into the spring, creating a small wave. I turned to face him, and he *mostly* kept his gaze on my face. He stayed near the side of the spring though, not invading my space, but he was already turned on if his erection was anything to judge by, not at all hidden by the clear water.

Still combing my hair with my fingers, I said, "I think I might cut my hair if I can find a way." Ilk groaned loudly. It was slightly alarming, and I raised my eyebrows at him as I flicked my wet hair over my shoulder. "Is that a problem?"

"I like your hair."

"I like it too, but it's knotty and messy and would be easier to care for if it were shorter. It'll grow quickly."

"But then you'll just cut it again."

I couldn't help it. I chuckled at how much it bothered him. "Well, yes." Ilk still looked devastated at the idea of me with short hair, and it was so cute I had to offer him an alternative. "I'll tell you what… if you can find a way for me to comb my hair and keep it knot-free, I'll keep it long."

"I'll find something."

"I bet you will," I murmured, smirking.

"I can braid your hair like mine."

I paused in my combing, having images of myself with long, luxurious braids. "All right."

Ilk watched silently as I finished bathing, and I didn't mind his wandering eyes. He was an intriguing combination of confidence and curiosity. Cautious around me so as not to scare me off, I imagined, but also flirty and playful. It was getting harder to imagine finding a life on this planet without him, and I could only hope he would come with me when I went to look for the other girls.

It was official. I couldn't handle the guilt anymore. I had to ask him now.

"Ilk?" He hummed, raising his eyes from my chest to my face. He wasn't cleaning himself, and I was curious to touch his body. He'd already touched me a bit, and I wanted to know what his skin felt like. Was it the same across his entire body? His chest was hard, muscled, and slightly textured, dappled like a newly painted wall. Did he feel like that everywhere? Distracted, I said, "You're not washing." Before he could answer, I moved over to him, snatching another gladvin root from the side of the spring. His gaze was glued to mine, and when I was right up next to him, another rumble worked through his chest.

"May I?" I whispered, holding up my hands with the liquid from the root on them.

Ilk nodded and growled again when I placed my palms on his chest, rubbing the oil over him and working over his shoulders and arms. Gently, he placed his hands on my hips and let me continue washing him. It was nice to be held by him—safe and comforting in a strange world.

"Ilk?" I repeated, and he hummed again. "I need to go find the other girls." His back stiffened at my words, but he said nothing. "We got separated when they released the pods. I need to make sure they're okay… they could be lost and hungry." I patted his chest with a small smile. "Maybe they didn't all find big rock alien men to look after them." Still, Ilk said nothing, but his gaze was sad. I cleared my throat. "Um… so I wanted to know if you would come with me and uh… help me search for them? I don't know this planet at all, and I only really feel safe with you."

"You want me to come with you?" His voice was hoarse, and I wondered if I'd somehow offended him.

"I mean, I'd understand if you don't want to leave your home, but I could *really* use your help. And we don't have to stay away forever. We can come back once we've found them. I'd just feel so much better knowing they are as safe as I am with you."

"You feel safe with me?"

"I…" I paused. *Isn't that what I just said?* "Yes, I feel safe with you."

His grip on my hips tightened. "I will go with you, Errrica." At the moment, his voice had become so gravelly, he returned to his original pronunciation of my name, and it hit me what an idiot I was. I wasn't offending him. He was *worried* I would *leave* him. Ilk wanted me to stay with him. It had been a few days, yet I knew if it weren't for the other girls and the potential danger they might be in, I would stay with Ilk in a heartbeat.

I threw my arms around his neck, launching myself from the water and hugging him. Ilk jolted, possibly alarmed by my attack, and I chuckled as he slowly wrapped his arms around my body, holding me against him, his face buried in the crook of my neck as he inhaled deeply.

"Errrica," he grumbled, and I felt his cock twitch against my leg.

"Ilk…" I whispered his name into his ear. *Was I going to tell him no or to keep going?* I wasn't sure. My body was reacting to him, and with the steam from the spring in my nostrils, his usually masculine musk was even more intoxicating. He inhaled the scent of my skin again. Hopefully, it was better for him now that I wasn't covered in weeks' worth of grime and sweat, and that familiar rumble moved through his chest.

Fuck it! If I'm going to go on a quest where I might die, I might as well fuck my alien man first.

"Ilk," I moaned out his name, loving the sound of it on my lips. "Can I kiss you?"

He drew his head back from my neck and studied my face, his bright green eyes flicking between my lips and eyes. "I know what you ask because I have your language. But Synths, we do not…"

"You've never kissed anyone?" Ilk shook his head, and I fought the urge to giggle, allowing only a slight smile to manifest. I wasn't laughing at him, but here was this giant alien, almost made of stone, appearing meek at the idea of kissing. He still held me around my waist so our faces were next to each other, and I lifted a hand from his shoulder and placed it on his cheek. "Just follow my lead."

He didn't move, staying stock-still as I moved my lips toward his. I smiled right before making contact—he was so cute. When he went cross-eyed, trying to watch me as I got closer, I laughed. "Close your eyes."

He did immediately, squeezing them shut as though he were expecting pain. I gazed at the adorable expression for a moment longer before pressing my lips to his. Straightaway there was the rumble through his chest, a long, satisfied note that lingered as I worked my lips on his. They weren't soft like human lips, but they weren't unpleasant either. I'm certain most of the stiffness was because he was pressing them together, unsure of what to do. His arms tightened around me as I flicked out my tongue, trying to coax Ilk into opening his mouth. When I ran my tongue around his lips, and he inhaled sharply, I took the opportunity and pushed my tongue into his mouth.

Ilk groaned again, and his large, flat tongue found mine, flicking over it playfully.

He was a fast learner. He had told me that, but I hadn't thought it applied to everything.

With one arm still around my waist, his other hand snaked up my body, his large hand grasping the back of my head as Ilk deepened the kiss. His hips were grinding against my body, his cock rubbing against my thighs as he pushed against me. *Holy fuck.* My thoughts were a mess. There was no way to concentrate on anything other than the overwhelming sensations that ripped through my body. His tongue against mine, the rumble of his chest with his contented growls, and the warmth of his body were only enhanced by the hot spring.

With a grunt, Ilk spun me around, lifted me onto the bank outside the spring, and the cool air whipped against my skin. My nipples immediately responded. Ilk groaned, laid me flat, wrapped his arms around my thighs, and buried his face between my legs, his hands over my breasts, massaging. He pushed his tongue inside me, almost as thick as his fingers, and I stifled my moan by jamming my arm against my lips.

With a snarl, Ilk grabbed my arm and wrenched it away from my face. "No," he growled out, squeezing my wrist. "Don't cover the sounds you make. I want to hear you."

He was back between my legs, fucking me with his tongue and every now and then coming up to lick and suck at my clit. I was a mess, completely coming apart under his touch, simultaneously nervous and excited about the prospect of going farther with him and how good the stretch would feel as he forced his cock into my pussy.

"I need you wet, Errrica," Ilk grumbled the words in between licks that drove me wild, "You're so small that I need you extra wet so I can fit inside you."

I simply moaned as he returned his attention to me, nodding my agreement but unable to form any words. I grabbed Ilk's head, holding him against me as I neared my peak, and with my legs shuddering and breaths coming out in staggered gasps, I came, crying out his name.

CHAPTER 16

ILK

There would never be a time when I would tire of her taste or the flush of warmth as she came on my tongue and mouth. Kissing her had been exquisite, and I simply needed to repeat the same motions on her sweet cunt, thrusting my tongue in and out. Ghaals didn't kiss, having more of hard, beak-like lips than Erica's beautiful soft ones. But kissing her was only trumped by repeating the motion with my tongue in her cunt.

Lifting Erica into my arms, I moved to the edge of the spring where the water was shallower and up to my thighs, positioned her so her legs were straddling me, and groaned again as she wrapped her legs around me, holding herself as close as she could get. Erica was light, and I'd be able to control how quickly I penetrated her.

If I could control myself that long.

Only when I was fully sheathed inside her wetness would I return us to the water, where she could feel weightless as she bounced on my cock.

Even the mental image made me moan.

Erica tightened her legs around my waist and pushed her tongue into my waiting mouth again. I understood the appeal of the kiss. It was a warm-up to what was to come, a show of the skills I had to please her, and the way she moved against me, her supple breasts pushing against my chest only increased the pleasure.

It was becoming difficult to keep myself together now that the scent of her arousal mingled with her intriguing natural scent, and I simply wanted to drive my cock up into her and make her scream with pleasure. I could feel a muscle twitching in my neck as I struggled to maintain control of the primal part of me, as I didn't want to hurt her. Erica trusted and felt safe with me, and I would do nothing to change that.

I wrapped her hair around my hand and used the leverage to break the kiss. Erica's pink lips were swollen from our kissing, and I groaned again. Her lust-filled eyes drank in my gaze, and slowly and gently, I lowered her onto me, the lips of her cunt stretching open to welcome me inside. So wet, so warm, the scent of her around me made me groan. I waited for the slightest hint I was hurting her, moving slowly into her.

Her small fingers gripped my shoulders as the tip of my cock pressed against the entrance to her tight cunt, and I had to use her weight as leverage to get inside her farther than the head. She was so tight and squealed as I snarled when my cock broke through the resistance and penetrated her. With patience that pained me, I stilled. "Are you okay?" I asked, doing my best to keep my voice steady but aware of the vibrations of my growling through my chest. So content, yet wanting more, the animalistic side of me demanded to be let out.

"Yes," she whispered, her lips so close to my neck I could feel her warm breath against my skin. Her little hips moved against me, desperate for more, and we moaned together as I sunk into her a bit farther. "Oh fuuuck…" she groaned out.

When I was seated halfway inside Erica, I stepped deeper into the water, pressing her back against the side of the spring and tucking one arm under her leg. As she spread her thighs for me, I pushed in a bit farther and glanced down. Through the clear water, I could see my cock sunk inside her hot cunt, spreading and stretching only for me. Her hips were making grinding motions against me, and I matched her pace, every thrust sinking in farther until I was fully seated inside her.

"Fuck, *Ilk!*" she cried out, her hands scrambled against my back.

"I've got you," I mumbled, holding her tighter against me.

She was panting, her eyes almost rolling back with pleasure. When she shuddered as I pulled out slightly and pushed in again, I almost lost control, ending the thrust with a rough shove that had her grunting as her back hit the side of the spring.

"Sorry."

"It's okay... it's okay." She was still panting, but slowly they were making way to moans, and I kept it slow for as long as I could maintain control over myself. When Erica's moans hit a new pitch, I snarled again and grabbed her ass in my hands, slamming into her.

All it took was a simple whisper from her, "*Fuck yes, Ilk,*" and I lost control.

Gripping her, I began thrusting harder, my hands squeezing her ass as I pivoted her hips to meet my every thrust, groaning at how she opened up to me every time. She was so wet and tight I didn't think I would last long. *How long had it been?* I couldn't remember. But I don't think I'd ever been with someone as tight, sweet, and fragile as my Erica. I would never get enough of her, and she took my cock so well. It was absolute perfection.

When her hand drifted under the water and she

started rubbing herself, I moaned again, thrusting harder, bouncing her tight cunt up and down on my cock until my peak was close.

"Come with me, Errrica." I couldn't help the growl in my voice. This was a part of me I had long suppressed, and there was nothing in this world that existed now beyond the pleasure of her tightness stretched around me. She moaned, the sound so sweet, and when she came, there was a flush of warmth around my cock.

The was a spark in the back of my mind, a reminder that she was delicate, and I didn't want to hurt her.

I was too close to slow down.

Shifting her weight, I balanced her in one hand, my arm snaking around her body and cupping her ass in my palm. Continuing to thrust into her as she came around me, I gripped the edge of the spring, the rock crumbling under my grip.

With a roar, I came and punched the side of the spring. My skin hardened around my hand and rock met rock, creating a small crater next to Erica's shoulder. I kept thrusting, and when I shifted her on my palm, she squealed against my chest, her hands running up and down my skin. My eyes closed, lost in the sound of her moans and squeals—delicious sounds I had never heard the likes of before and never wanted to be without again. Coupled with the soft splashing of the water against the edge, my thrusts slowed, having emptied my seed inside her cunt.

"Ilk," she squeaked. She was panting again, moaning and squirming on my hand. My eyes still fluttered as I struggled to keep them open, the pleasure from my orgasm lingering. "Ilk, your finger!"

Her voice was somewhere between hysteria, amusement, and arousal, and I was snapped from my bliss to focus on where we touched. Erica was still squirming against me, the sensation making my cock harden farther inside her cunt.

But my finger, with my earlier adjustment, had slipped into her ass.

"I'm sorry, Erica," I mumbled, my cock twitching as she gripped around me, "It was an accident."

"It's okay, but can you take it out, please?" She moaned loudly as I shifted my hand, and I stopped moving, my eyes widening. She looked at me, her legs still wrapped around my body, held up only by my hands and cock inside her. She was at my mercy. I shuddered. "Why did you stop? You can take your finger out now."

"You... *moaned.*" I could barely string the words together, my tongue suddenly too heavy for me. The idea that she was turned on by my finger inside her while I fucked her cunt was too much. Was this something humans did often? It served no purpose for mating, but if it pleasured Erica, I wanted more.

"I mean..." Her cheeks flushed, and she fidgeted against me again. "It's uncomfortable, but it also feels kinda good."

"I didn't think both sensations could occur together."

She giggled quietly. "Neither did I." Erica squealed with alarm when I readjusted her, and instead of moving my hand away, I pushed my finger farther into her ass. "What are you doing?" she cried.

"Testing a theory."

"Ilk! Ilk..." Her shock died down as I pulled my cock from her cunt and began rubbing my shaft between the lips of her cunt, hitting the nub that brought her so much pleasure with every thrust. I used my finger to gently fuck her ass, moving only slightly in and out with each motion, and using my body, I pressed her against the wall so my cock was grinding against her.

"Do you think you can come like this?"

"Do I think I can come?" She was incredulous, her hands gripping me harder. "I can barely fucking think straight... fuck!"

Erica's orgasm approached quickly, so sensitive from the last two, and I rolled my hips against her, balancing her with my hands and keeping my finger buried deep inside her hot passage. I'd never even thought about this, and the thought of bringing Erica to orgasm again made another growl rumble through my chest. Her hands gripped my biceps, barely able to encompass the muscle, and as she shuddered and cried out when she came, I stilled my hand but continued to grind my cock against her clit, drawing out her pleasure.

"Holy fucking shit, fuck, *fuck... God!*" she cried, her head falling back against the edge of the spring as I pulled my finger from her and cradled her body against mine.

"Can I assume that series of words together is a good thing?"

She chuckled and adjusted herself so she was tucked against me. "Yes, a good thing, a very, very good thing."

I sighed, pushing myself away from the edge and into the deeper water, cradling Erica against my chest and letting the warm water soothe us. Her leg twitched intermittently, and I lowered my face to her hair, breathing in her delicious scent.

I would help her search for her friends. Given the danger she was in from the Ghaal, it made sense that we started to move and kept moving.

Maybe we would have to stay away from my cave as I was too close to the colony. Alone it was no issue, but with Erica, I couldn't take the risk.

We would journey together, and hopefully, we could make some stops along the way to revisit this pleasure.

CHAPTER 17

ERICA

So much better than I'd expected.

I wasn't even sure what I had expected, but it certainly wasn't three orgasms in a row, one from his mouth, one with his cock inside my pussy, and a third with his finger buried in my ass.

The initial stretch of his cock had been a lot, but he took it slow, being so gentle with me, even though I could feel his heart pound against the inside of his chest and his ragged breathing as he struggled to maintain control.

But when he let go of that control and unleashed, *fuck me,* that was something else.

I was a bit sore but not complaining as we drifted

around the spring together, naked and silent, simply basking in the afterglow of world-shattering pleasure.

A pang of guilt hit my chest as I thought of the other girls again. The idea of them wandering lost while I got fucked in a hot spring shuffled some of the pleasure away, and in my sadness, I pulled myself closer to Ilk. He didn't ask why, but simply wrapped his arms around me tighter as we drifted gently through the water.

"Ilk," I whispered against his chest, spluttering slightly when the water level reached my chin and a rush of warm water filled my mouth. He shifted so I was a bit higher and simply looked down at me. "Um…I want to go looking for my friends as soon as possible." When he didn't speak, I added, "Today, maybe. Early this evening. God, right now if we can. I'm worried about them, and I can't wait any longer."

"We will go tomorrow."

"But—"

"We have to plan our route, and depending on the direction, maybe gather some food to bring. I will braid your hair, and we will discuss where each unit may have landed. We will go tomorrow."

He was right, of course. I needed his knowledge of the planet. I only had a vague idea of where the pods may be. It made sense to me to go for the closest one first—*the forest, I think*—but he would know if that was indeed the best idea. Only Ilk knew what the food and shelter situation would be like, and we may need time to gather supplies.

I nodded. "Okay, tomorrow."

"Tomorrow," he repeated, snuggling his face against my hair again. He was obsessed with my hair, and I giggled. I wasn't the giggling type, so why was this alien reducing me to a giggling mess?

Oh, that's right, the mind-blowing orgasms.

"Well, shall we start getting ready?"

"Soon, Erica. I'm not done with you yet." My lip twitched into a smirk as he said my name, noting he said it perfectly most of the time, but when he was aroused, he always drew out the 'r' in that delicious growl.

"Oh, Ilk..." I patted his chest. "Um... I don't think I can so soon... you're really big."

He shushed me, inhaling deeply. "Don't worry, Erica. I will lick your cunt until it feels better."

How could I say no to that?

Hunting was not something I thought I would've considered doing. *Ever.* But then again, I never thought I'd be abducted by aliens and stranded on a strange planet, either. Ilk insisted hunting was necessary. Although there seemed such a wide variety of plants on this planet, I found it hard to believe it wasn't possible to survive on a plant-based diet. I was neither vegan nor vegetarian on Earth, but then again, I didn't have to venture out into the wild and spear my dinner with a pointed stick, either.

But I trusted him to know.

I still had a lot of questions for Ilk. I wanted to know where he came from. He spoke of his creators when pushed, or the few times they came up in conversation naturally. His creators were beings of advanced enough technology to create a synthetic organism capable not only of independent thought but emotions and desires.

So how did Ilk end up living in a cave with no technology to speak of?

There would be plenty of time for questions on our journey. Ilk estimated the walk to the denser parts of the forest would take two to three days, and I'm sure his estimation was based on me. I would need to stop for the nights and breaks during the day, not to mention I moved slower than he did. I wasn't prepared for him to sling me over his shoulder and carry me the entire way, but I'm not sure how long my resolve for independence would last if we hit some difficult terrain.

Then there was the next problem—once we were in the forest, we had to find the pod. My certainty that I had seen it fall into the trees dwindled with each passing hour. What if I were leading us on a wild-goose chase? But it was the best we had to go on. The ocean was two days in the opposite direction, but Ilk said we would have to skirt around the base of the mountains rather than walking in a straight line, which would add time, and Ilk seemed hesitant to go in that direction at all. It reminded me, when I'd originally left his company, how Ilk had steered me away from that side of the mountain. Another question I would need to ask him.

When we were discussing which pod to go after first, I again mentioned the one that had gone over the mountains. I had no idea how big the mountain range was, but if there were a chance that one of the girls was just around the corner, it would make sense to go for them first.

"If she landed on or near the other side of this mountain, she will be safe."

"Oh, apart from the pits of lava, you mean?" Ilk simply looked at me, and I sighed. "I'm sorry, that was uncalled for. But how can you know *for sure* she'll be safe?"

"Because my brother would have found her."

I held up my hands, halting his movement as he sharpened his spear on the rocky ground. "Hold up, your *brother?*"

"Yes. Lanir will find her. He would have seen the

units descending as I did."

"Do the pods drop often?"

His gaze was steely. "Too often. But I'd be lying if I said I wasn't glad you were brought to me."

Cute. But that raised even more questions. I sat next to Ilk and picked up the smaller spear he was making for me, mimicked his movements, and sharpened it. "How many siblings do you have?"

"Five."

"Are they all brothers?"

"We are whatever we need to be. We were created as male, but if we needed to breed, we could change. We choose to stay male. It's dangerous for us to live as female on this planet."

"Why?"

"Because…" he trailed off.

He had ceased his movements and looked off into the distance, over the ridge where he told me not to go. I followed his gaze. "Ilk, what's over there?"

"Before we go anywhere, Erica, I should tell you how you came to be here."

"Wait, you *know* why I'm here?"

"Please don't be angry. It's difficult to talk about, and we've been learning about each other."

"That's one way to put it," I mumbled, to which Ilk offered a lopsided grin. "Okay, I forgive you for not telling me before, on the condition you tell me *right now,* and don't leave anything out."

His eyes narrowed, but he nodded. "My creators live over that ridge… the last colony of Ghaals on the planet."

"Ghaals?"

He repeated the name, and I tried again to pronounce it, but I couldn't get the correct sound between the G and the H, so Ilk just waved a hand, the pronunciation was not important. "They are a violent race with advanced technology. After almost wiping themselves out, most of them set off to find another planet to colonize, and those who remained searched for a way to increase their numbers."

"What's stopping them from just breeding?"

"Fertility issues, a side effect from the chemical warfare."

"So they created you and your brothers, the Synths?"

"Yes, we were designed to be adaptive, strong, and able to breed with the Ghaals as we were created based on their DNA." He held out his arms, and my gaze automatically traced his body. "I look like this because I live here. Over time, my body adapted to my environment."

"That's incredible." Although I knew what his skin felt like, I still ran my fingers over his arm. He felt and looked like living stone because he lived within the rocks. Fascinating.

"How did you end up here?"

"My brothers and I left. Once we realized what the Ghaal were like, we decided we did not want to help save them. We split up, so we wouldn't be tempted by the part of ourselves that is designed to breed, and we spend our days directing others away from the Ghaal colony."

"So the pods?"

"There are other species, from other planets, who are facing extinction for a variety of reasons... disease or war. Some scour the galaxy for compatible species, some do it peacefully, and others... do not. Some see certain species as below them, no more than animals who don't have rights and can be used as objects for breeding."

I wrapped my arms around my stomach, feeling sick. "So..." I swallowed heavily. "My friends and I were going to be used... for breeding?"

"Yes. The Moeks who took you have a deal with the Ghaals. Any species they take that is not suitable for them, they will drop here, and the Ghaals can try."

"Oh my God." Ilk reached out and touched my shoulder as I swayed where I sat.

Used for breeding by an alien species, I think I was going to be sick.

I remembered being on the ship. "The aliens who took us, the Moeks, they... looked at us, inspected us..." I shuddered and pulled my arms tighter around myself, "...and they didn't seem to like what they saw."

"You were not compatible with them. Despite their belief, they have the right to kidnap other species, but the Moeks are generally peaceful. If you were not compatible without surgery, they would not proceed. The Ghaals, on the other hand…"

"What?" I whispered the word when he paused, barely able to find the strength for any volume.

"They will find a way to breed…" Ilk said, his expression stern, "… by *any* means necessary. As their numbers dwindle with every passing generation, they become more desperate."

"Will they come looking for us?"

Ilk paused, and I searched his eyes for an answer. "Possibly."

I knew he really meant *yes*. "Ilk, tell me the truth."

He took a deep breath, and I almost wanted to tell him not to tell me. Whatever it was that had him so rattled that he had forgotten the spear in his hands and could barely look at me, maybe I didn't want to know. "There were others before you."

"Other species?" I knew that. He'd just told me.

"Other humans."

A sharp pain shot through my chest, and I clutched at it. *Other* humans? *We're not the first?*

Images of being strapped to those white tables while my legs were forced open and being impregnated in a lab filled my mind. I shuddered, and tears squeezed from my eyes, which Ilk gently wiped away. "We have to find the other girls," I pleaded, looking at him desperately. "I can't have them get caught by the Ghaals."

"This is why my brothers and I are across the planet. Lanir and I are closest to the remaining Ghaal colony. We steer away all life forms that drop in the units, either by scaring them or communicating if we can."

"That's very noble to sacrifice your own chance at a life to protect others."

He lifted a shoulder, his face earnest. "It's the right thing to do."

His protective nature and intelligence made me want to kiss him.

But we had work to do.

CHAPTER 18

ERICA

It was late, and Ilk was finishing braiding my hair before we went to sleep. We had gathered some water and weapons to carry with us on our journey, and Ilk assured me that food would be in abundance, so we didn't need to bring much with us. He was still insistent I hunt, and I supposed I wouldn't be able to resist forever and only hoped he started me with something small.

The corner of my lips twitched.

Start me off with something small, indeed.

Get your mind out of the gutter, Erica.

I had packed some of those root berries in a pouch in case we found a place to bathe. I had drilled Ilk about this, and apparently, there were streams around, but we would need to find a safe one. *Bathing came second to survival*, he said, and I'd rolled my eyes. *Duh,* I'm not going to risk my life for a bath. But I wanted the berries anyway, so I had something sweet to offer whichever girl was in the pod that headed toward the forest—a peace offering, something to feed them and quench their thirst if they needed it. I wanted to be prepared if we found her.

When we found her. I wouldn't give up until we had.

Then we would find the next.

Ilk's reassurances that his brothers were living around the island—*the largest land mass on the planet,* he said—helped ease my stress, but it was a big place, and even twenty alien men around may not be close enough to where the pods landed, let alone six. Even searching for them blindly was a stretch, but I had to try. Searching with Ilk by my side, I at least had a chance and wasn't simply wandering off to my death.

Ilk's fingers worked well with my hair, finer than his, and he tied off each braid with a leather strap until there were around a dozen braids, which he then pulled back and braided together into one. I reached back and ran my hand over my hair when he was done, impressed and glad I wouldn't have to deal with knots for a while.

"Thank you," I said, fingering the end of my new hairstyle.

I was seated between his legs while he kneeled behind me, and Ilk leaned forward, breathing in deeply near the crook of my neck and making me squirm and giggle when he released the breath. "Now you can keep your hair long for me."

"What's your obsession with my hair?"

"Before I lived in the mountains and my body changed, I had more hair," he mumbled, running his hands up my arms and making me tremble. I had removed my cloak and was wearing only my pants and the strip of fabric around my chest. "I like it. It's very sexy." He leaned forward again, this time brushing his lips against my neck. "And don't think I didn't notice the little tuft of hair between your legs. Mmm..." he grumbled out another growl, and I chuckled. Good to know he found it so attractive because I certainly had no way of shaving or waxing anymore.

Turning, I placed a hand on his chest. "We should get some sleep."

He watched me for a moment, his green eyes blazing. "When can I have you again?"

"I..." The desire in his eyes was all-consuming, and I don't think anyone had ever looked at me like that in my life. The logical part of my brain told me we needed sleep because we had a long day of walking tomorrow, but that part of my brain seemed to lose out every time he was close.

"May I fuck you again tonight, Erica? Do you want your little cunt stretched by my cock again?"

"Holy hell... um... I mean, I do..."

May I fuck you? Holy shit. Such a politely phrased question shouldn't send my mind reeling as it did.

Ilk pressed his lips to mine without any force behind the motion. I could pull away and tell him no, that it was time to sleep, and he wouldn't ask again. But for some reason, this alien man was irresistible to me, and when I parted my lips to allow his tongue to play with mine, he lifted a hand to cup my breast, and we moaned together.

He took his time with the kiss, but every flick of his tongue became more frantic as he laid me down and undid the knot of the fabric under my breasts, continuing to massage me. His skin was deliciously textured against my nipples, and I undid my pants and pulled them down, kicking them off with my feet while his hands were otherwise preoccupied. With a pull of a thread, he ripped his loincloth away, discarding it as he settled between my legs.

Opening my legs for him, I sighed at the weight of him on top of me. He didn't let me take all his weight, but he was so large all I could see was him as he held himself above me, still massaging my tongue with his. When he reached between my legs and ran a finger up my slit, I bucked my hips when he reached my clit.

Ilk grumbled again, a low satisfied hum. "You are already wet for me, Errrica."

So soon, I was going to take that monster cock inside me again twice in one day. I must be insane. Did I forget I had hours and hours of hiking to do tomorrow? That I had to hunt, set up camp, all the things I had zero experience with on Earth, let alone here?

But then he rubbed my clit in circles, and I did forget, and I could barely think straight without release.

When I began thrusting my hips against his hand, Ilk dipped a finger inside me, snarling when I moaned. He was usually so gentle, intelligent, and well-spoken, but when he touched me, it was like there was an animal underneath that came to life. He said he was created for breeding, so it must be *me* that brought it out in him.

I felt a certain level of pride at being able to make this hulking alien man come undone.

My thoughts were interrupted when he repositioned himself and lined his cock up with my pussy, pushing my legs open farther to accommodate his body. He pushed forward, and I squeezed my eyes shut, the stretch so consuming I couldn't concentrate on anything else. He trailed one hand down my side and under my ass, lifting me against him, and used his other arm to keep his weight from settling fully on me.

I clutched onto his shoulders as he began rocking against me, grunting with every thrust that pushed him deeper inside. God, I could come just from this—the gentle rocking of him. I was so turned on by his presence alone I felt I was on the edge of orgasm from the moment he started touching me.

Ilk's slow ministrations didn't last long, and the animal came out to play once again.

With another snarl, he pushed forward until he was fully inside me, and I cried out with satisfaction. His thrusts were wild and harder than when we were in the hot spring, and all I could do was clutch his back and hold on as he fucked his cock into me. Every time I moaned, his growling would start anew, a constant rumble in his chest that vibrated against my nipples. His grip on my ass tightened, and his growls turned feral as he got closer to his release. When I moved to snake my hand between our bodies, he slapped my arm away, changing position so he was kneeling and held one of my ankles in the air. When he started rubbing my clit, my fingers scrambled for purchase against the cave floor, my eyes rolling back as he forced me closer to my peak.

"Oh fuck, *Ilk!*"

I came around him, and he kept rubbing my clit until the waves of my orgasm lessened. He then slammed his fists onto the floor on either side of my head, pounding into me at a brutal pace, roaring loudly as he came, and I felt the warm rush of his clear cum soak my pussy, squeezing out around his cock.

Ilk dropped to his forearms, encasing me with his body, his head buried against my neck. "I love it when you cry out my name, Errrica."

"I love that little growl you do when you say my name when we fuck."

He growled again, ending with a small chuckle before he pulled out and wrapped me up in his furs and held me against him. I listened to the sound of his breathing, his heart rate slowing as he came down until I fell asleep, safely tucked against him.

Ilk poked my shoulder, and I grumbled, grabbing the furs and rolling over, pulling them over my head. "Just five more minutes." There was a deep chuckle before the furs were ripped from my grasp. I squealed as sunlight assaulted my eyes, and I threw an arm over my face.

"We must go. The sun has risen," Ilk said and stalked off to the other side of the cave and gathered our supplies together.

"All right, all right." Fucking alien, chirpy in the morning. I went outside to relieve myself and swallowed a few gulps of water before I snatched up a strip of the bark from a moobark tree. We'd had some yesterday, and watching Ilk rip the bark off, grunting as he did so, showed me he either had no idea I wouldn't be strong enough to do so, or he was messing with me the first time. His short, flat teeth ground the rubbery bark into nothing quickly, but I found the only way I could eat it was to nibble the top of it with my incisors like a rabbit, slicing it into fine enough bits to swallow. It wasn't an unpleasant flavor, vaguely nutty, but my molars did nothing but bounce off the damn stuff.

Okay, so maybe some meat wouldn't go astray.

I slung my cloak back on and picked up my spear, accepting my water bag from Ilk, only a third the size of his. He carried another small bag with some of the root berries in it at my insistence, but otherwise, we would gather food along the way.

Looking down at my body and again running my hand over my braided hair, I felt almost like a warrior princess or something. I had a spear, tough clothes, and a badass hairstyle that was practical but also awesome, and it filled me with a sense of confidence I'm certain would be wiped away after a few hours of hiking.

"Hi... *YA!*" I swung my spear out in front of me, and placed one foot firmly in front of the other before attempting a high-round kick that was more like a thigh-level swing.

When I turned with a huge grin on my face, Ilk was watching me with a startled expression. "Is this... some sort of human custom before a journey?"

A light bulb went off in my mind, and I decided it was time for my revenge for him setting me up with the bark on those damn trees. "Yes. It's a sacred dance to bring good luck over long journeys."

Ilk seemed pleased and let me teach him my best half-assed Bruce Lee moves. I made it through three rounds before I broke down laughing at the sight of this giant gargoyle-esque alien going *hi... YA* and swinging his spear around.

As I clutched my stomach, Ilk straightened, a deep frown furrowing his brow. "There is no sacred dance?"

"No," I huffed out, breathless from laughing. "I'm only sorry I couldn't keep up the charade long enough for you to do it in front of your brothers." Ilk seemed unimpressed, but his lip twitched when I approached and patted him on the chest. "Lighten up, big guy. It's payback for you telling me I could tear the bark off that damn tree."

His grin told me all I needed to know, and he didn't deny it had been a setup. I shoved him playfully, which did literally nothing. I might as well have shoved the side of the mountain, and we set off over the rocky ground.

Away from the Ghaal colony and toward the forest to search for the first girl.

CHAPTER 19

ILK

Erica was worried more than she was letting on. While she was playful and joking, the moment her laughter ended, the slight frown would once again adorn her face. She'd then pout and scan the horizon around her from the ocean in the distance to the mountain we stood on and finally to the forest where we were headed. I admired her desire to reach her friends, even though she had told me they'd never met prior to being abducted and had only limited communication on the Moek ship. They were bound together by circumstance, and Erica would not be able to rest until she knew they were safe.

I hoped they were safe.

I had confidence in my brothers.

When they saw the units, they would have moved toward them as I did, and I'm sure they would have realized not only the girls' vulnerability to this planet but how much the Ghaal would want to claim them.

But I understood Erica needed to be sure.

My plan was to take her to the forest, and while it had been a long time since I had sought out my brother, Vitri, there, I knew roughly what part of the forest he resided in. This would limit our search area and increase our chances of finding the second human female. If Vitri hadn't found her already, then he would help us search.

We couldn't stay with them, though. I hadn't told Erica this yet. The more of us gathered together, the easier it would be for the Ghaal to get to the females. We needed to keep moving, not staying in one spot for more than one cycle of the moon. This wasn't the life I wanted for Erica, but it was the best I could offer her for now. We'd make sure her friends were safe, then we'd figure out where to go from there, and I could only hope she wanted to stay with me.

As Erica and I began our walk, I thought about my brothers while keeping an eye on Erica. She stumbled over some of the rocks but was able to right herself without falling, even though my hand shot out automatically to catch her if she were to fall. Every time, she would offer me a small smile, and my heart would swell.

I worried my feelings toward Erica were more than simply instinctual.

But that would have to wait.

My appearance had changed much since I was created. Originally, we resembled the Ghaal more closely, with grayish skin still tinted with a hint of a scaly pattern from an ancestral trait no longer required and thick purple fur down our backs and arms. But the Synths' eyes were always green instead of orange, and I never knew if the Ghaals designed us that way on purpose so we could never quite blend in or if it were purely an accident. Cooler colors of blues and greens were considered weak in Ghaal culture, where reds and oranges represented power and war. Perhaps if it were intentional, it was to remind us that we were inferior to them.

Or so they thought.

Vitri has been in the forest for as long as I had been at the base of the mountains, and I suspected we would not look much alike now at all. I ran my hand down my braid and draped it over my shoulder. Maybe, like me, he kept this reminder of who we once were as the rest of his body shifted around him to adapt to his new environment.

Lanir resided on the other and markedly more

dangerous side of the mountain, where it was plagued by potholes that reached deep into the mountain, filled with lava that bubbled up to the surface on occasion, darkening the terrain further as the fire the soil breathes hardens and sets every rainfall. There was no danger of an eruption as I had needed to reassure Erica several times since I first mentioned it. The small volcano in the mountain did not build enough pressure to erupt, instead spewing forth the lava through small pits on the other side. Lanir would also look different, having to adapt to the heat and danger of the area and to blend in where streaks of red-hot lava spilled down the side of the mountain.

With Lanir being where he was, my stance in my cave, and Sahcor by the oceans, we had the Ghaal colony mostly surrounded and were able to ward off most of the abductees from the Moek units. I had other brothers near too, and the farther from the Ghaal colony, the more spread out we were. Our planet was made up of only two islands that wound their way around the planet, so one of us was never too far from the coast. Ghaals remained here for the abundant food and fuel sources, and we were always close. I imagined since the remainder of the Ghaals had abandoned the planet, the second island would have been completely taken over by nature. This pleased me, and I was glad it was being left alone to thrive at its own pace, uninterrupted.

Perhaps these human females were to be our saviors.

I had never considered that Synths should breed to increase our numbers, but while we lived long, we were not eternal, and there may be merit in considering growing our population. If the females wished to stay with us, if Erica wished to stay with me, perhaps we could start a family.

But then again, maybe the human females would wish to start their own colony together and not be near the Synths at all. The idea saddened me, and while the pain settled heavily in my chest, I said nothing because I had known a life of protecting others, and there was no reason I couldn't go back to such an existence. If a few short days or weeks was all I was to have with sweet Erica, and if she wanted to go and make her own life, then I would not stand in her way.

As long as I continued to keep her safe from the Ghaals, then I would be happy.

Happy enough, at least.

The time passed pleasantly, and I slowed my steps to keep pace with Erica. The farther we moved away from my cave, the more determined she appeared, and our rest breaks became fewer and farther between. At our last stop, we refilled our water bags in a small stream, Erica grumbling about how much easier this was than rainwater caught and perched high on a boulder. I chuckled, but I preferred the water back home. The water from the rain was fresher and not tainted in taste by the fallen leaves and roots from trees upstream.

The rocks from the mountain floor had made their way to fields and scarcely wooded areas that stretched and dotted intermittently between us and the main forest. As we moved away from the mountain, there was more wildlife, most of it harmless. There were small flying tipids that ate only seeds and flowers and some game that could be hunted when we were hungry. The fields were too open for much else. Predators stayed within the wooded and forest areas, where they could hide and stalk. I could see Erica ached to stop and look at things, but then she'd cast another worried glance at the forest and keep moving, craning her neck to see whatever creature we had just passed.

Sometimes, she couldn't resist.

"Ilk?" she asked, and I looked at where she was pointing. "What the hell is that?"

I thought she was going to ask about the oarke. Maybe there was a herd in the distance. They were large creatures we used for furs, covered in a shaggy teal coat that blended in with the forest and hide strong enough to make excellent leather. But I stopped when my eyes adjusted to the landscape. So many times, my vision glazed over these things, and I no longer really saw them.

But the remains of what was the Ghaal civilization when it was thriving and powerful still lingered across the planet. Now in a state of disrepair and overgrown with lush flora, the abandoned buildings and wreckage were visible if you were looking for them.

The black metal, odd angles, and straight lines stuck out against the wild bliss of nature that surrounded it. "That was part of the Ghaal city when it existed."

"What was it, though?"

I squinted. By the time I was created, the civilization had been reduced to a single community. It looked too big to be a home since most of the Ghaal preferred to reside near the coast. "I can't be sure. One of the larger buildings, perhaps for supplies, maybe to create weapons."

"Wow," Erica muttered, staring at the wreckage for a moment longer. "They really fucked themselves over, didn't they?"

I simply grunted. I didn't want to talk about the Ghaal anymore. "Tell me about your planet," I said after a pause.

Erica huffed out a laugh before hitching her water bag higher on her shoulder as we began walking again. "You might need to be more specific than that. There are so many things to talk about, I wouldn't know where to begin."

"Okay." I thought for a moment. While the idea of human culture intrigued me, what I really wanted to know was more about Erica herself. "Describe your residence to me."

"I live in a house made of bricks," she started, and I was able to tally up definitions of these words as she said them—a building created from small blocks made from clay from their soil, not so different from what the Ghaal had used in the beginning, until the materials made from nature made way to man-made substances as their technology increased. "Except, I don't own the house."

"Who does?"

She lifted a shoulder. "I rent it from someone else. Some people can afford to buy many houses, and the ones they don't live in, they rent out to other people."

I narrowed my eyes, trying to understand. This only raised further questions about the workings of the financial system on Earth, and that wasn't territory I was particularly interested in exploring. Not right now, anyway. We had time to talk about anything we wished, and maybe if we got really bored, we could cycle around to the financial system of her home planet. "I want to know what your home looked and felt like, Erica. Not the logistics of who owned it."

She threw me a look, then smirked, brushing her fingers along the inside of my forearm, sending a tingle up my spine. "Sorry, not used to answering these sorts of questions." She paused for a moment, looking around at the field as she collected her thoughts. "Okay, so in my room, I have a bed and a *really* soft mattress, the kind you sink into when you lie on it. Then I can pull my blankets over myself and my pillows and be cocooned in warmth." She sighed, wrapping her arms around herself briefly as if remembering the sensation. "The blankets are pink. They *were* bright pink but are faded now. Not my first choice in color, but they were on sale. They were the first thing I bought when I moved out on my own, and I'm kind of attached to them now." She smiled, then the smile dropped. "At least, I was. None of that stuff seems particularly important now."

"It's important if it means something to you."

Erica smiled at me and slipped her hand into mine. I gripped her palm, closing my fingers around hers. "Are you unstable on the ground?"

She laughed. "No. I just want to hold your hand." When I continued to look at her, she added, "It's a comfort thing like... showing affection."

"Oh." I squeezed my fingers gently around her

hand again. "I like it."

"Me too."

As the sun lowered, Erica's steps slowed. She was dragging her feet, leaving long trenches of bent grass as her boots scraped along. Her lips were pressed together in a thin line, and she stared determinedly ahead. Any conversation we had about comparing our planets had died off hours ago when exhaustion had started to set in for her.

"We need to find a place to set up for the night," I suggested, scanning the area.

"No, we can keep going."

With a few well-planted steps, I caught up to Erica, placing a hand on her delicate shoulder. "Erica, you don't need to prove yourself to me. You'll be no good to your friend if you pass out from exhaustion."

She stopped, reached up, and patted my hand.

I surveyed the area again and located a small ridge of rocks in the near distance. There were many of these around the fields, becoming fewer the farther we moved from the mountains. This one would suit us well as we could have our backs to the rocky structure and not be approached from behind. We were far enough away from the wooded areas that I doubted we'd have any trouble tonight, but Erica was a stranger in these lands, and I needed to take every step to keep her protected.

When I turned around, Erica's shoulders had drooped, and her eyes were closed. She appeared about to collapse onto herself. With a snarl, I scooped her up, hooking an arm under her legs and carrying her. She was immediately alert. "What are you doing?"

"You're exhausted. I should have stopped us hours ago."

"I wanted to keep going. You can't control everything, you know."

"I can't control *you*, you mean?" When I glanced down at her, she was smirking, although she had settled into my arms.

"Yes, that's exactly what I mean." She huffed, not bothering to hide her grin.

Her playfulness made me want to take her again, but she was tired and needed rest. I already harbored guilt from fucking her last night too long when I should have let her sleep. But now that I'd had her, my ability to resist touching her was ebbing away, giving up in lieu of a more primal part of me.

As I set her down against the rocks, I gazed out over the field. "I need to get us some dinner."

"I want to come."

"Erica, you're tired. Just stay here."

She was on her feet, up against me with her warm and tempting body, her hands pressed against my chest as if she knew I wouldn't be able to say no the second she touched me. "Please, Ilk, don't leave me alone here."

Snarling, I grabbed her arm. "Fine. But I will carry you."

"How... oh!" She squealed as I lifted her over my shoulder, swinging her around so she could wrap her legs around my waist and hold onto my neck.

Snatching up my spear, I ran, and Erica squealed again, first in fright and then laughed as I thudded across the field. There would be a herd of gorae around here somewhere. The fields were full of them—white and gray furry creatures with six-pointed hooves and horns that could be painful if they got near you. They wouldn't attack unless threatened, so the trick was simple—strike first.

I slowed as I spotted a herd in the distance and pointed them out to Erica.

"Oh my God," she cooed. "Look at them. They're so cute with their fuzzy little faces and big eyes. Hello, baby... *Ilk, what the fuck?*" she screamed as my spear went through a gorae's neck, and I lumbered toward my kill. It was a quick kill, merciful, and I wouldn't have it any other way.

Picking up the animal by its rear legs, I carried it back to where we would make camp. Erica sniffled behind me. "What's the matter?" I asked.

"You killed it."

Her voice was small and broken, and I didn't understand. "Yes, we need to eat. Do humans eat their meat while it's living?" The thought made me ill, and I felt Erica shaking her head against my back.

"No, no. I guess I wasn't expecting it."

"We needed to hunt."

"But it was so… cute."

I struggled to figure out what her concern was and how this might relate to human culture. "Do humans only eat ugly animals?"

"Well… no."

"Erica, I'm trying to understand."

The patience in my tone apparently increased her frustration. "I just… I didn't want… it was just *cute*, okay?" She said this as though it explained everything, and I didn't ask further questions. Erica squealed again as I swung her off my back, and she landed on the ground with a little *oof* sound that made me smile. I set about stripping the fur from the gorae so I could cook it, and Erica turned her back.

When I was almost done, I turned to find Erica peering over my shoulder. Her face was whiter than usual, and her eyes widened. She swallowed when she caught my eye. "I guess I should learn how to do this, right?"

"I will teach you."

When I lifted the carcass, she held her hands out, palms up to halt my movement. "No, no. I'll just watch you this time… and maybe next time too." She swallowed again, mumbling, "And maybe the time after that as well…"

I studied her for a moment. She was so strange. Adorable but strange. "Okay."

When the animal was free of fur, I built a small fire, found a flat stone to put on top, and threw the meat onto the stone, the sizzling sound perking up Erica instantly. Her stomach grumbled as she watched the gorae cook. "Okay, so maybe I was hungrier than I thought."

"We've eaten only plants all day. Of course, you're hungry."

"You know there are humans who live only on plants." I eyed her out of the corner of my vision, trying to figure out if this was another *cultural dance* joke. She caught my look and chuckled as I turned the meat. "I'm serious!"

"I believe you."

I didn't, not quite, and she smirked as if she knew.

When the gorae was cooked, I ripped two legs off and handed one to Erica. She took it delicately as if it were going to come to life and attack her before taking a tentative nibble of the meat. My pride swelled when she hummed in delight and took a larger bite and chewed gratefully. I took a leg for myself and bit it in half.

Erica stared at me. "You eat the bones?"

I stopped midchew and returned her stare. "You don't?"

"I don't think I could."

I eyed her small teeth. Yes, they would probably break. I lifted a shoulder as I finished the leg, then chuckled to myself. The act of shrugging was still strange and one of the few mannerisms I had picked up when I connected with her mind. I tried to think what action we had that was equivalent and realized there was none. If faced with something we didn't know, we would tell you or just stare.

"Nothing goes to waste," I said, watching her. I would wait until she had her fill before I had more.

"That makes sense." Erica was happily chewing away, and I was pleased I could provide for her. "I have another question for you." She looked at me, and I waited for her to continue. "If the Ghaals had the technology to create synthetic organisms, and intelligent ones at that, how come you live in a cave and have to hunt and make fires?" When I opened my mouth to answer, she kept talking, and my lip twitched into a smirk. She either talked a lot or not at all. There seemed to be no middle ground. "I mean, I understand that you and your brothers separated yourselves from them. But couldn't you have taken some technology with you? Build yourselves homes, maybe weapons..."

Erica let her words trail off, and I fought to keep my expression neutral. But it was too late, and she had seen the anger burning behind my eyes. I was not angry at her, and it was not her fault she didn't understand.

"We didn't want their technology." For something to do to keep my hands busy, I snatched another leg. There was still plenty of meat left for Erica. "Their technology, their science, all their weapons, all they ever did was make it worse for themselves. They simply couldn't resist the pull of the power, and they had to have more. More power, more destruction." I shook my head. "When we left, we left all of that behind." Taking a shuddering breath to steady myself, I glanced over toward the direction of the colony. I couldn't see it, but the knowledge it was there was enough to send bolts of anger through my chest. "When they were almost wiped out, they lost the ability to repair their technology, and most of the specialists had left the planet in the purge. Their colony is in disrepair, and they have limited technology left. I wish they had lost it all... then perhaps they could learn to be peaceful."

"I'm sorry," Erica whispered, looking down. "I didn't mean to make you angry."

I wondered if somewhere, deep down, she was still afraid of me. It didn't take much to note the size difference between us and the dissimilarity in strength. If I wanted to, I could kill her or hold her against her will. I hoped she understood that I didn't want to and would never hurt her. But boiled down to the truth, she was on a strange planet with a being completely alien to her. Erica put her trust in me because she had no choice, but I wanted to *earn* that trust.

"I'm not angry at you. Please don't be frightened of me."

Her gaze shot up to mine. "I'm not frightened of you..." but then her voice became small, and she looked down and tentatively took the final leg from the gorae carcass, her eyes traveling over to my spear before resting on me again. "I don't need to be afraid of you... right?"

Dropping my meat back on the hot stone, I moved over to Erica. She watched me approach as I shuffled closer. Erica gripped the leg of the gorae in front of her, but she didn't flee. I settled next to her, touching her chin and lifting her head so she faced me. She closed her eyes, her lips slightly parted as if expecting a kiss, and as much as I wanted to fuck her mouth with my tongue, that wasn't why I came over next to her.

"Look at me, Errrica." I let out a growl and watched as her eyes fluttered open, the brown hues of her irises dancing in the light from the fire. "I will *never* hurt you."

Her pupils flicked back and forth between mine

and over my face. "I believe you."
   I hoped she did.

CHAPTER 20

ERICA

Ilk had held me last night, pulling me close against his body after extinguishing the fire. He said it was unsafe to leave it burning all night, and when the winds he had warned me about picked up and began whipping my clothes around my body, I understood why. It wouldn't be good to have embers flying around when we were surrounded by exceptionally flammable fields.

When I struggled to sleep, Ilk tucked me behind his back so I was against the rocky nook and his hard muscles so I could keep warm. I blocked out the sounds of the wind as best I could by tucking my head down and lifting my cloak over my ears, snuggling as close to Ilk as I could get. He chuckled a few times as I readjusted, and I wondered if he was ticklish.

Wouldn't that be something? A ticklish gargoyle man. Definitely worth testing at some point.

As the sun was rising, we kicked soil over the remnants of the fire, and after I took a quick break to relieve myself behind the rock and then splashed some water on my face, we set off again.

The aching in my feet came sooner today. These fur boots were comfortable for sitting around in the cave or on small walks to the springs, but they were not suitable for long hikes. However, my choices were these or no shoes at all, and since Ilk had made them by hand specifically for me, it would be ungrateful to complain. His feet were large, flat, and calloused, even though he wore boots of his own. Perhaps over time, my feet would toughen up.

Hopefully, I would toughen up in general.

Why did I never consider learning survival skills? Because I never thought I'd need them.

Ilk asked questions about Earth and humans as we walked, and I also pointed out things we passed. We came across more introduced species than native, and I seethed at the idea that Ghaals had been kidnapping creatures from near and far for years, trying to save their sorry asses. Ilk said that some creatures didn't last long, and others ate weaker native creatures, many of which were almost wiped out by the chemical wars to begin with. But eventually, everything found its place in an equilibrium that was interrupted every time new pods dropped.

The forest was starting to come into focus now, and it was encouraging to see what was a green blur finally appear closer and take shape, individual trunks of trees formed with every step I took. Ilk thought we should reach the forest edge this afternoon but still wanted to stop for the night outside the forest before venturing inside. I didn't argue since he knew what was best. Now we were closer, I noted what originally appeared to be a large mass of green now contained a blanket of multi-colored flowers and plants under the green canopy of the trees.

"Are all those plants native to the planet?" I asked, picking up my speed slightly to walk next to Ilk.

"No. Sometimes seeds get brought with creatures who land here... in their fur or maybe in their digestive system. As with the wildlife, the plant life here is a mix of native and introduced species. Some have been here so long I couldn't even tell you if they were here from the beginning."

"Ilk..." He hummed as I did a quick double step again to keep up. When he looked down at me, he slowed his pace. "Have you had any humanoid creatures here before?"

"Humanoid?"

"Humanoid, like you and me." When he continued to stare at me, I waved my hands about. "Two arms, two legs, two eyes. Humanoid."

"There have been some, yes, but few I could communicate with as well as I do you."

"So, wilder, then?"

"Yes, I suppose that term makes sense. Maybe they were just afraid of me."

I was about to say that's ridiculous. Why be afraid of Ilk when he's so gentle? But letting my gaze sweep over his body, I reminded myself of how intimidating he was and how frightened I was of him when we met. It seemed like weeks since I was cowering against the rear of the cave, on the verge of wetting myself every time he got too close.

Left to my own thoughts, I focused on the forest and all the details that presented themselves clearer with every step. As the hours passed and we neared, some of the flowers had explored beyond the canopy of the forest and out into the field, blurring the lines between the two landscapes. There was a flower that reminded me of the flowers on passionfruit vines on Earth, but it was many times larger, about the size of a tractor tire. As we walked past it, I stopped to look.

"Ooh, this is pretty."

Ilk grabbed my arm as I reached out and

snatched me away from the plant. "Stay away, Erica."

"Why? Is it poisonous?"

"Yes. It will also lure you closer to it with its scent, and when you are close enough, it will release poisonous barbs. Then your rotting corpse will fertilize the soil above its roots."

"Lovely. That's just... lovely. Wait..." I turned to Ilk. "How does it *lure* me in with its scent? I'm not an idiot, and I won't go *oh that smells nice, better go shove my face in it.*" As I said it, I realized that was exactly what I was about to do.

"Pheromones, like mine. It makes it irresistible."

Okay, everything he said led to more questions, and I frowned at my feet before looking at him again, my expression hardening as my thoughts gathered. "What do you mean pheromones *like yours?*" I held up my fingers and did air quotes around the words, forgetting he may not understand the gesture.

"I was designed to breed, Erica. I have a strong pheromone release."

He said it so matter-of-factly like it wasn't a big deal. My jaw dropped as thoughts swirled around in my head. I needed to remember that Ilk may be alive, but he was a synthetic organism designed for a purpose—to breed, lure females, and *fuck.* If he had pheromones, exactly how strong were they? Even as I was trapped in my thoughts, his scent washed over me, almost making me weak at the knees. The feeling was quickly replaced by anger.

"Is that why you smell *so* damn good to me?" I demanded.

Ilk moved toward me, scooping his arms around me and burying his face against my hair. "You smell good to me too."

I pushed away from him, and he released me, his brow furrowed. "No, no, hold up just a second." I started pacing, reliving all my interactions with Ilk. From the very beginning, he smelled amazing and made my head spin whenever he was near. It was an effect that was enhanced until I could no longer resist him, and we had fucked in the hot spring. "Am I attracted to you *because* of your pheromones? I mean, can I overcome them if I didn't want to be affected? Or are they so strong I wouldn't have any choice? These aren't some normal chemicals but were created in some alien lab. Have I been under the influence of some *come-hither-and-fuck-me* drug?"

Ilk's face changed when realization dawned as to my not-so-subtle implication. "You always had a choice." The words ended in a growl, and I wasn't sure if he was mad at me or himself.

"Did I? Because right now it kinda feels like you drugged me with your organic-synthetic-lab-created-masculine scent and fucked me with your *equally* lab-created *alien dick!*" I know I was getting worked up, but everything that was happening was a fuckload for anyone to deal with without the sense of betrayal that was creeping up my spine. Ilk was the only being I could trust. He'd saved me and looked after me when I otherwise would be no better than dead. The idea that my response to him and any bond we'd formed was purely chemical—and he *knew* he had that effect—sucked whatever messed-up romance was in this interaction right out of it.

"Errrica—"

"No." I held up a finger. "No, no. I need a minute to think." As I moved to walk away, Ilk went to follow, and I spun on my heel, rounding on him. "I need a minute to think, Ilk. Please leave me alone."

And without a backward glance, I stormed into the forest.

There are a few things I know for sure in this life.

One, the whole *expect-the-unexpected* thing absolutely *does not* prepare you for some of the wild shit that life might throw your way. I expected an unexpected bill or an unexpected visitor. Like a stopping by for coffee visitor, not a visitor from another planet on a mission to kidnap me to use as a breeding machine.

Two, I know I shouldn't have wandered into a potentially dangerous forest alone on an unknown planet.

But it was difficult not to see Ilk as at least a little bit of a monster. Physically, he could simply take me and keep me captive, and the fact that he didn't had some merit. But the idea that he was fully aware I would have a chemical reaction to him and said *nothing* grated against me.

"Hey, Errrica," I mumbled, mimicking his deep voice the best I could while I stomped through the undergrowth. *"Just a heads up, I smell fucking amazing, and it's going to drive you wild and make you want to take my giant alien cock."*

Scoffing, I kept moving.

Perhaps on some level, I knew Ilk would protect me. Maybe he was only a few feet behind me, somehow able to hide the rumble of his heavy steps when he wanted and move silently, keeping hidden in the shadows. That would account for the boldness of my pace, and that I kept moving even when, at one point, I was certain I felt a vine creep around my ankle, and my immediate reaction was to stomp on it and stab it with my spear. But then again, I had told Ilk to leave me alone, so maybe he wouldn't have thought I'd go too deep into the forest without him.

Dammit! It was hard to stay mad at the big lug.

But I needed space and some time to think.

For the most part, I had been along for the ride—and enjoying a great deal of it since being able to communicate with Ilk—but eventually, this shit was going to catch up with me, and I needed to get my head on straight.

Finding a tree with large roots that dove in and out of the soil, creating a tangle of deep green trunks across the forest floor, I found a spot and sat, leaning my back against a higher root and looking up toward the forest's canopy. There were more animal sounds here, chirrups and chirping, the occasional growl and scuffle, things that could be attributed to life that was absent near the mountains and the Ghaals. Taking a long, steadying breath, I wanted to close my eyes and drift away with my thoughts, to take a moment to mourn for the life I had lost and would never get back.

But I would do my mourning with my eyes open because I may have been foolish enough to wander off into the forest alone, but I certainly wasn't going to sit here with my eyes closed.

It was almost peaceful.

My peace was broken when I heard crashing through the undergrowth. I looked around and had two choices. Hide amongst the large winding roots or climb up a tree and get a good vantage point.

I chose up.

Scrambling to get sturdy footing, my boots

scuffed against the mossy-like bark as I found footholds, finally able to pull myself onto a low branch and eventually a bit higher.

The crashing got louder, and I released a breath when Ilk shoved two tree trunks apart with his forearms, looking around. "Erica?" he cried. If it weren't for my residual anger, I'd feel almost bad for the big guy.

He took a deep breath.

Dammit! Could he fucking smell me?

His pace slowed as he stomped across the forest floor, ripping up roots as he searched for me. He knew I was close and wouldn't be able to keep this up for long. But I was still angry, and while I knew I would go to him and continue our journey, I wanted him to be upset, even if just for a little while. Call me petty, but when I say I needed space, I *needed space.* He should at least respect that.

Eventually, when Ilk had torn up half the forest floor around the tree I lay in, he looked up, a snuffle ending in a snarl, leaving his lips as he straightened. Ilk shook his head as if trying to gather his thoughts as much as I had and walked farther into the forest.

When the sound of his heavy steps had died away, I slid down from the tree. I'd go and wait for him outside the forest, where we'd had our... disagreement. Even if we couldn't talk it out, I would need to push it to the side because we were here to find whichever girl was in the pod that had landed around here.

Stepping over the large roots, I tripped, and my scream was muffled as a hand was slapped over my mouth, and I was dragged behind the tree.

CHAPTER 21

ERICA

Struggling against the arm wrapped around my torso, I gripped my spear and lifted it, slamming it into the foot of the perpetrator. He cried out, a strange sound that almost appeared to echo within itself and let me go. I didn't bother to look back and took off the way I had seen Ilk go, trying desperately to leap over the roots knowing if I tripped on them, I'd be as good as dead.

There was crashing behind me, and my breathing became panting as fear mingled with exhaustion from our hike all day. My heart felt like it was going to burst, and I wouldn't be able to keep this up for much longer.

Whatever our current qualms, I needed Ilk.

He would protect me.

As I opened my mouth to scream for him, I was tackled to the ground, and a hand once again slapped over my face to keep my screams at bay. Wrestling with my attacker, I caught a glimpse of orange eyes and gray skin as we rolled before I was slammed against the forest floor and my arm twisted behind my back.

Hot breath hit my ear. "Silence, I'm trying to help you." I stilled, mumbling something against the hand over my mouth, his skin smelling like rancid cherries. He spoke again, "If I release my hand, do you promise not to scream?" I nodded against the leaf litter and thick moss on the ground, and there was a grumble over my shoulder. "I'm not sure I believe you, and although I'm trying to save you, I really must be sure you won't attract the attention of the Synth. How about this? If you scream, I'll hurt you so you *can't* call out. Understood?"

I nodded again with more frenzy and gasped when he released his hand but kept me pressed to the ground with my arm twisted. "How can you speak English?" I asked in a rush.

"The Moek transport units are infused with the language of the species within. You would have been scanned the second you stepped inside. I simply downloaded the information."

"The second I was *pushed* inside, you mean?"

He huffed out a breath. "That was… regrettable, but I need you to listen to me now. The Synths are dangerous, and I need you to come with me."

"What? I don't believe you. Who are you?"

"My name is Rah. I am from the Ghaal—"

"You're one of them!" I took a breath to scream for Ilk, and the hand was slapped over my mouth again. I tried screaming anyway, but it was too muffled for Ilk to have heard me.

"You've been lied to, female, and I need you to come with me."

I shook my head rapidly until he released his hand. "What do you mean *lied to*?" I hissed out.

"I don't know what you have been told, but we created the Synths… that much is true. But it is not us kidnapping species and bringing you here, it is the Synths. They have almost wiped us out and intend to breed an army to rise against our remaining numbers."

"Why should I believe you?"

"Let me ask you this, human. You've been here a matter of days… have you already had sex with the Synth? Did he use his pheromones on you?"

I stilled, hating what I was hearing and refusing to answer. Ilk had been nothing but kind to me since I landed on this godforsaken planet, and despite the pheromone debacle, I found it difficult to believe he had been using me this entire time. If he was creating an army, why would he live in a cave alone and away from his siblings? It seemed a huge charade to hold up just in case someone like me came along.

There was a hum behind my head. "You're silent because you're thinking it through, and you know I'm right."

If the Synths could change gender, why would they need to kidnap females to breed?

"No," I whispered, tensing my arms and steeling myself. "I'm silent because I know you're full of shit. *Ilk!*" I screamed Ilk's name with every bit of air I had left in my lungs.

The Ghaal behind me roared and grabbed a handful of my hair, wrenching me from the ground and dragging me backward.

"This is what I get for trying to do things the peaceful way. Stupid idea, Sol." He was mumbling under his breath, not concerned with my struggles as I grabbed his wrist and tried to loosen his grip on my hair. Rah maneuvered me until my back was at his chest and slapped a hand over my mouth again, hissing against my ear. "This would've been so much easier on you if you had just come with me." I cried out as he dragged me over a root that snagged on my pants, ripping through them and cutting into my leg. "But the good news is we don't have time to return to the colony tonight, which means you get to spend the night with my scout group in the forest. They're very keen to meet you."

I tried to cry *no* against his hand, but the cry was lost, and I struggled to keep up with him as I was dragged sideways through the forest.

Oh God, Ilk, please find me.

ILK

However angry Erica may have been with me, none of that mattered when I heard her call my name. It wasn't a playful call.

I would have even preferred to hear anger still in her voice, and for her to be shouting my name in rage.

I would have preferred anything to the fear I heard.

And even as it sent a shiver down my spine, I turned and bolted, crashing through the undergrowth and tearing trees out by their roots if they got in my way as I headed toward where I had heard her cry. There was nothing to be found apart from a few broken branches from a scuffle and a strip of leather that looked like it was torn from Erica's clothes. Roaring with rage, I dropped to my hands and knees and inhaled deeply, like the animal

I was becoming because my female was taken from me. I smelled her in the soil and the definite sickly scent of the Ghaal. Releasing another roar, I bolted forward, not bothering to move with any level of stealth. No, I wanted them to know I was coming and tremble with fear as the ground shuddered with my approach.

I wanted them to know I was going to tear them from limb to limb if they so much as laid a hand on Erica. There was no need for technology or weapons since I was seeing red and would need only my bare hands.

Slowing my pace as Erica's scent became stronger, I stopped and turned on the spot. "Erica!" There was no answer to my cries, and my chest was heaving with each breath, ragged and angry snarls ripping through me with every exhale. I could smell her. She was so close it was like she was standing right next to me, but I couldn't see her. Lashing out wildly, I tore up more trees, swinging my arms around and pulling apart the forest in my wake. She was here somewhere. I knew she was, and I would tear this place apart until I found her.

As I shredded the forest and there was still no sign of her, I realized I must have been wrong. Maybe they lingered here for a moment, and that strengthened her scent. Erica was so ingrained in me, her scent so close and on my skin from all the times I had touched her, that maybe I wasn't thinking straight. I took a few steadying breaths, although my shoulders still shook, turned, and made my way farther into the forest.

Right now, I needed to find my brother, Vitri.

He knew these forests as well as I knew the mountains, and he would help me search.

No matter how long it took.

CHAPTER 22

ERICA

He was right there, my Ilk. I could see him, and if I weren't being crushed against the chest of the Ghaal who kept me captive, I'd be able to reach out and touch him.

But he couldn't see me.

The air shimmered slightly between us, an effect from the cloaking device the Ghaal had used when he heard Ilk approaching. Both of us hidden, he had jammed a scrap of fabric in my mouth and slapped his hand over the top, and I couldn't make a sound above a muffled whimper. Ilk was crashing through the undergrowth, destroying everything within arm's reach as his nostrils flared. He could smell me, but he couldn't see me no matter how long he searched. Tears sprung into my eyes as Rah dragged me farther backward while Ilk's circle of destruction increased. After what felt like an eternity, Ilk stopped and closed his eyes before moving off into the forest. I cried out a muffled sound against the gag as he disappeared from my sight and sobbed, allowing myself to be dragged away from the site by Rah.

I couldn't lose hope.

Ilk wouldn't give up on me.

He only went to get help.

He wouldn't leave me with the Ghaal.

Images of being strapped to a table and impregnated with strange tools filled my mind or of creatures like Rah, the Ghaal that held me now, leering while moving on top of me, his orange eyes glowing and sickly gray skin moving against mine. I choked back another sob, drool leaking out the sides of the gag as I cried openly. Rah seemed unconcerned with my cries, and when I stumbled over a root, he simply yanked me to my feet, ignoring my muffled cries of pain as my ankle twisted.

I wanted to be in a better frame of mind, to be strong, and plot my escape, but a sense of hopelessness I had been able to hold back while I was safe with Ilk now filled me. Every strange plant we passed would have looked beautiful and fascinating in Ilk's company was now simply a vivid reminder that I was incredibly far from home and in very real danger.

We reached a small group of trees, and as we got closer, I couldn't get my eyes to focus on them and blinked rapidly, thinking I was being drugged. But no, the trees themselves were slightly out of focus. If I weren't being steered toward them, I wouldn't have noticed, walking straight past without seeing anything off. I began to struggle anew as we neared the gap between the trees, and Rah hissed out something in his native language, a series of syllables that made no sense with an emphasis on G sounds and intermittent clicks, and shoved me toward the gap.

Stumbling, I fell between the trees and, throwing my hands out, landed on a cool, gray floor. Scrambling to my feet, I wasted no time and threw myself back the way I came, only to slam into Rah's chest, who grabbed my hair and snarled in my face. I answered with a muffled scream, hoping to sound at least a touch threatening, but he used my hair to maneuver me around so I was in front of him and marched me down the hallway toward the doors at the end.

Before we reached the doors, they slid open, jolting slightly halfway before disappearing into the walls as we were met by another Ghaal. He had his palm flat against the wall next to the doors and simply watched us approach, expressionless. The walls were pockmarked as though rotting, and the lights dimmed and flickered, although I couldn't see the source of the light.

The place was falling apart.

Good, I hoped it turned to dust.

"Great idea, Sol," Rah said as we got closer. "This little bitch didn't fall for it." He shook me for emphasis, then sneered in my ear. "She thinks she's so damn smart… she didn't fall for your idea for a peaceful recovery of the cargo, so I had to take her by force."

I screamed against my gag again, and Rah chuckled. The Ghaal, Sol, watched me as Rah shoved me forward into his grasp, his face still blank. He hissed out something at Rah in their native language, and this was followed by a heated exchange between the two. Rah then glared at Sol and turned, disappearing into a hidden door in the side wall, and I was left alone with a new Ghaal.

He watched me, his large brownish pupils surrounded by the thin ring of bright orange, studied me, and looked almost… *sad.* I stopped struggling and held his gaze, and even as he reached up and pulled the gag from my mouth, I gratefully wet my lips and then simply watched him back.

"Please," I whispered, looking back to make sure the hidden door Rah had disappeared into was still closed. "Please, let me go."

There was definitely a sadness in Sol's eyes this time. "I tried to help," he said, his voice gravelly and thick, like he was speaking through a bubble. "I tried to get them to take you peacefully."

"I don't want to be here." I was crying now, the tears streaming down my face thick and fast, and I couldn't bring myself to do anything about it. "I don't want to be used for breeding, please. I want to go home." It struck something in my heart when I realized when I said *home,* I meant back to Ilk and not back to Earth. Being with Ilk had felt more like home than I had felt on Earth in a long time. *Surely, those feelings of safety can't all be pheromones?* I should have asked Ilk about them more rather than overreacting. But now, I may never get that chance. Ilk said I couldn't go back to Earth, and I believed him. I didn't even question it. And here, surrounded by aliens with greater technology, I didn't even care to bother asking.

I wanted home.

I wanted Ilk.

Sol said nothing.

"Please," I said again, aware of how desperate I sounded and hoping if he had any semblance of emotion inside him that it would strike a chord. "Please let me go." Sol grabbed the back of my cloak and shoved me forward, and although his touch was gentler than that of Rah's, he was still leading me farther into the Ghaal lair and not to freedom. Panic gripped my chest. "No, Sol. Please, *please!*"

He stopped, spun me around, and slammed my back against the wall. "This is not easy for me, female, do you understand? I grow weary of the way things are being done here." His eyes flared with intensity, and I shut my mouth. "Be quiet, or I will need to gag you again."

Any hope I had felt dissipated from my body, and I sunk under the weight of my fate within this building as I let Sol steer me away.

Sol nudged me into a cage.

Unlike the ones on the spacecraft, these had visible bars made from something that was so cold to the touch, it was almost like being burned when I grabbed them. Yanking my hands from the bars, I watched Sol as he diligently locked the cage, moving his fingers through the air near a silver ball on the door, which was followed by loud clicks and clanks I assumed of a mechanism moving into place. As with the larger door, the sounds were jolted as though the locks struggled to move properly. Maybe they were old and almost broken, and I could break them if I could see *where* they were.

"Sol?" When I said his name, he looked up, his

hand still hovering over the silver ball. Keeping my voice low, I asked, "What did you mean… *you grow weary of the way things are being done?*"

He continued to stare at me, and I jumped back when he blinked, his eyelids moving in from the sides instead of up and down. I took the moment of silence to study him, and I could see why Ilk was so concerned about my safety and how interested the Ghaal would be in me and the other girls. We were eerily similar, and aside from skin and eye color, their intimidating height, and the placement of hair on their body, we shared the same shape, build, limbs, and similar hands. Although Sol's palms were larger and flatter than any human I'd ever seen, he had the same number of fingers as Ilk, one less on each hand than me. When I pictured aliens, I always imagined shapeless blobs, but the similarities in our evolution were fascinating.

At least, it *would* be fascinating were I not in a cage on a strange planet.

I desperately wanted to know if they already had the other girls captured, but couldn't bring myself to ask in case they didn't know about them. Maybe they thought *I* was in the pod that landed in the forest, and that's where they'd gotten the language from. If that were the case, then the girl who was *really* in the pod might still be safe, and I would not be the reason she got captured. So, despite the need to know eating at me from the inside, I kept my mouth shut.

We had passed a handful of cages before Sol put me in this one, and they were all empty. I allowed myself an iota of hope that it meant the other girls were still free. Then I had to hope they were safe, wherever they were.

Sol blinked again, and I managed to refrain from flinching this time. "You are not the first species to be taken."

"I know," I muttered, scowling. "The Synth told me."

"What else did he tell you?" I pressed my lips together in a thin line and offered nothing. Sol tilted his head slightly down. "I understand you don't trust me... I can't blame you." He looked back toward the door we had come through, and his hand was still hovering over the silver ball. "Whatever he told you, I imagine it's all the truth. Synths never were much for lying."

"Sol," I whispered his name again, and he looked at me with such sadness I almost felt pity for him, despite me being the one in the cage. "The Synth's pheromones, do they..." I swallowed, it seemed so unimportant right now, but I needed to know if this longing I felt for Ilk was real or simply the result of a chemical reaction brought on by his design.

"You quite like him, don't you?" I shut my mouth again, a purposeful action that wasn't lost on Sol, and something almost resembling a chuckle left his hard lips. It wasn't a pleasant sound, nothing much about the Ghaal seemed pleasant, but maybe I was biased. "To my understanding, the pheromones that emanate from the Synths are an aphrodisiac only. They aren't a drug as such and can't make you do anything you don't already want to do."

"That's what he told me." My voice was less than a whisper, drowned out by the realization I had thrown my safety away over a tantrum and hurt feelings that could've been resolved if I had only stayed by Ilk's side and let him talk to me.

When I said nothing further, Sol raised his hand to the bars as if he wanted to touch me in a reassuring manner before he looked at the floor and dropped his hand to his side. "I'm sorry," he said, turning to leave.

"Sol," I said, but he didn't stop, and desperation gripped me again. I grabbed the bars, ignoring the burning cold, and shook them even though they didn't budge. "Sol, don't leave me here! Please. *Please!*"

The door slid behind him silently, and I was alone with the sound of my pleas echoing off the walls.

CHAPTER 23

ILK

"Vitri!"

I called for my brother every few steps as I moved farther into the forest, swatting low limbs out of the way rather than bothering to duck under them. I was barely containing my rage as it was, and every small break of a limb helped soothe the anger for a moment before I would think of Erica again, and it would bubble to the surface and threaten to consume me. But I couldn't save Erica if I threw myself around like a wild animal. I needed to concentrate and think logically, and I knew Vitri would be able to help me.

The forest extended for many days farther this

way before meeting the mountains that curved around the island. But I was certain that Vitri was only a couple of hours into it and closer to the side that trailed around the edge of the mountain ranges where I lived as they dipped and sunk into the plains. I could only hope he had maintained his original post as I had, and I cursed that we hadn't thought to keep in more frequent contact to make sure we knew exactly where to find each other.

But it had been many years, and how were we to know that things would play out as they did? How long had the Ghaal been hiding out across the island? Were we so blind as to miss them moving about? I'm certain any camps they set up across the island would not have the technology needed to artificially inseminate the females—I remembered those rooms. The technology required simply to transport the table would be too obvious. So it seemed they are perhaps camping around the place, waiting for units to drop, and getting to the occupants before we could.

How were we to know?

"No!" I punched a tree, the anger igniting in my chest as it snapped in half with a satisfying crack. There was no excuse. We *knew* that one day they would find compatible females again, and then it would be up to us to protect them from the Ghaal. We didn't think ahead and became complacent, and now Erica was suffering because of my stupidity. I would do better. *I would do better* and promised myself that we would do everything in our power to put an end to the Ghaal.

If only I could save Erica first.

The animalistic part of me she had awoken roared to life now, and I leaned over, grabbing a tree and ripping it from the ground, its roots pulling up soil and smaller plants as I straightened. Slamming it back into the soil, the trunk gave way and splintered before it shattered.

"Vitri! I need your help!" My voice boomed throughout the forest. No echo came back to me, and no response from a voice I knew I would recognize the second it came to me. The forest had a way of dulling sounds. Rather than my shouts moving across the plains or bouncing off mountains, they were absorbed by the lush plant life. This is why predators resided here—sneak attacks were easier.

I kept moving.

The sunlight became only a dappled memory as the canopy thickened, my way lit by thin streams of bright light that filtered through the lessening gaps in the leaves. Erica would have wanted to stop and admire the scenery, and a growl rumbled through my chest at the thought. I would show her the forest once I rescued her.

Another bout of anger and another tree was ripped from its roots.

Any predators in this forest were unlikely to approach with the noise I was making. It would be too loud and foreign, and they would flee.

I heard a squeak of fear and spun so fast I almost lost my balance. I knew that sound. It was the sound Erica made when she was afraid. But when I turned, I found myself facing another human female. Her skin was darker than Erica's, and her hair was so black it was almost the color of the shadows, cut in a short style that stuck up around her ears. She was clothed in furs, a thick strip wrapped around her chest, long enough that it was almost a dress. Her dark eyes widened as my gaze traveled up and down her body before settling on her face, and her fingers gripped her spear as her eyes found mine.

She turned to run, and I lunged for her, grabbing her ankle as she slammed to the ground, kicking out at me before I grabbed her other foot. When she twisted her spear around and attempted to jam it into my thigh, my hardened skin made the assault useless, and her spear broke on contact. She screamed even as she kicked out at me, trying to loosen my grip on her legs as I dragged her toward me. There was a hint of guilt in my chest at frightening the human, but I had to ask.

"Erica," I growled out, grabbing the woman's shoulders and hoping her language was the same as my Erica's. "Have you seen Erica?" She stopped kicking and stared at me, her eyes widening further.

But she said nothing and tried kicking out again after a moment of shock. I dragged her until she was under me and held her still with my body weight. She continued to squirm, and then I got too close, and she snapped at me with her teeth, almost biting my face. I snarled. She was a fighter, I'll give her that, but I didn't have time for this.

"Where is Vitri?" I thundered, and she made a squeak of fear again, sinking back against the forest floor.

She opened her mouth to speak, and my hope spiked.

"Vitri!" Her cry was piercing, and I looked up in time to see my brother barreling toward us. I grunted as he collided with me, his shoulder hitting my ribs and rolling me off the female on the ground. I wouldn't have recognized my brother had I not been prepared to see him. The environment of the forest had changed him as much as the mountains had changed me.

I grabbed his wrists, and when vines snaked out from his back and started to bind me, I snarled out. "Vitri, it's me. Ilk."

His green eyes flashed with rage, but the creeping vines stopped their progress around my arms and torso. "Ilk?" His voice was softer than I remember, but perhaps I had simply gone so long hearing only my own. Slowly, realization dawned across his features, replacing the anger that had flared in his eyes a moment earlier.

Vitri lifted himself from me, and after only a moment of hesitation, he held a hand out to help me up. He stumbled slightly under my weight when I pulled myself to my feet, and his lips lifted into a smirk as he took in my appearance.

"Rock boy," Vitri scoffed out, a grin planted firmly on his features.

Rock boy?

I glanced at the human female, who glared at me and then poked Vitri roughly in the small of his back. "What are you doing? This ass attacked me. I thought you wanted to protect me, and you're just letting him go?"

Vitri reached out to grab the woman, and she leaped out of his reach, glaring at him instead. Vitri was still smirking, and I watched the expression dance across his face. I tried to remember what he was like before we separated, and I do recall he was often joking before we were faced with the reality of our makers. Of my brothers, Vitri was the one I was the closest to, but it was still odd to see him so cocky, back to his original self, I guess. It had been so long I'd forgotten who he truly was, much as I had forgotten myself. It seems the human female had had the same effect on Vitri as Erica had on me, bringing out a side of him long lost to a solitary life and duty.

When she danced out of his reach again, the

vines from his back lashed out, wrapping around her wrists and waist and twirling her toward him. She cried out in anger, struggling against the grip of the vines, which were released the second Vitri scooped her next to him with an arm possessively around her waist. She started beating at his chest with her palms, and I frowned. Maybe they weren't as close as Erica and me. It seemed the affection between them was definitely one-sided.

Vitri wrestled with the female until he had her wrists firmly in one of his hands and held her arms above her head as she continued to wiggle. "This is Tori," Vitri said, turning to me. "Tori, this is my brother, Ilk."

"That's fucking fantastic. Let me *go!*"

Vitri released her with another chuckle as she spun out of his grasp.

Tori lifted the broken half of her spear, prodding me in the chest with the splintered end. "What do you know about Erica? What have you done with her?"

Vitri's brow furrowed. "Who is Erica?"

"Another human female," I said. My heart was thumping in my chest at the thought of her. "The Ghaal took her in this forest. We came looking for you," I added, narrowing my eyes at Tori. She seemed angry and ungrateful, and it was Erica's concern for her that put her in this forest in the first place. Tori's expression softened as her eyes widened in fear. I can only assume that Vitri had told her the truth as I had Erica. Looking back at Vitri, I continued, "They must have camps set up now, waiting for the pods before we can steer the species away. They were expecting them this time, Vitri. They must have been to be so prepared. Erica is my mate, and we have to get her back."

"Your *mate?*" Tori's voice was small, and she tossed a glance at Vitri that I couldn't read. "What makes her your mate?"

"I claimed her."

She threw another look at Vitri, eyes widened, and he replied with a smirk. I broke the silence with a roar of frustration. "Are you going to help or not?"

"Of course, I'll help," Vitri answered, not bothered by my show of rage and aggression. "Then we can find the other humans, yes?"

Tori threw her arms up. "That's what I've been saying!"

Vitri smirked again. "Only because I said it first. An excellent idea I had."

Tori huffed out in frustration but said nothing as a growl rumbled through my chest. I didn't have time for this. We needed to find Erica *now*.

Vitri clapped me on the back with an open palm, and my shoulders stiffened. But his smirk had vanished when we made eye contact, and his tone turned serious as he said. "Can you show me where she was taken?"

I nodded, and before we turned to leave, Vitri rounded on Tori, who stopped midstep. "Go back home and wait for me."

"Ex... *cuse me?*" she said, pressing her hands to her hips in a gesture so reminiscent of Erica I groaned quietly. "You are *not* the boss of me."

Vitri closed the gap between them in a handful of steps and swooped down to grab her shoulders, lifting the woman off her feet so they were face to face. "The Ghaal are dangerous, Tori, and despite what you think of me, I care for you and your well-being. I will help save your friend, but please, *go home.*"

Tori searched his face before nodding, and when he placed her gently back on her feet, he turned, only to stop again when she reached out and touched his arm, twisting the small vines around her fingers. "Be careful, okay?" she whispered.

Vitri held her eye contact before nodding, and together he and I moved back through the forest.

CHAPTER 24

ERICA

Awaiting my fate, I had decided I was tired of sitting around, and although my one escape attempt on the spaceship had been a failure, it wouldn't stop me from trying again here. Because, unlike last time, I had an ounce of hope to cling to—there was someone on the outside looking for me, someone who wouldn't give up until they found me.

Rattling the bars did nothing, but it made me feel better to take out some of my rage on them. When I realized I was doing nothing but wasting energy, I moved around the cell, inspecting every inch, every corner of the cold room, searching for the tiniest hint of weakness.

There was none.

I couldn't even find where the locking mechanism was. There was nothing I could pick and prod at to figure out how to open it. The locks had made sounds, but otherwise, there was no sign of them. Peering up and down the hallway lined with cells, I sighed. There were no guards and, therefore, no one I could try to trick or attack. Hell, I'd even attempt to use my feminine wiles if I needed to— anything to get out of here and back to Ilk.

Hours passed, and the door at the end of the hall was so silent I didn't even realize it had opened until I heard the footsteps of a group of Ghaal approaching. They came to a stop outside my cage, chattering excitedly between themselves. I backed against the far wall, not liking the way their eyes roamed my body.

One of them was shoved forward by the others, and with an unsettling grin, he hovered his flat hand over the silver ball, the clink of the locks releasing before he entered my cell. I had only a split second to debate if I should run at the group or back into a corner, and for better or worse, fear got the better of me, and I backed away. The door closed behind the Ghaal, and he glanced back at his companions, all laughing appreciatively as he approached me, his hands out and fingers curled, ready to grab me.

"Get away from me!" I cried, backing against the rear wall. This only brought on more laughter from the group. I skirted around the corner of the wall as he got closer, and in my desperation to escape, I ran around the cell, only to be grabbed through the bars by the Ghaal outside my cage. I kicked out and screamed as hands found my body, pulling my arms back and holding me still until more hands found my legs. I was trapped against the bars, and the Ghaal inside the cage with me approached calmly.

Even as tears streamed down my face, I still spat at the Ghaal who stood in front of me. His smirk turned to rage, the orange of his eyes flaring before he slapped me. The force of it would've knocked me off my feet if I weren't being held upright. My struggles continued as the tie on my pants was undone, and they were yanked down. When my bare ass pressed against the burning chill of the bars, I cried out and tried to get away from the pain, only to have the Ghaal laugh louder. The Ghaal before me bent down and inspected between my legs, slapping between my thighs until the ones on the other side of the bars got the hint and spread my legs for him.

Apparently, he liked what he saw, and I cried with fear and humiliation as the excited chatter increased. He hovered his hand near the apex of my thighs, his finger outstretched, and I squeezed my eye shut, whimpering.

Abruptly, I was let go, and in my hurry to get away from the bars, I tripped over my pants and landed hard on the floor. There was an explosion of laughter behind me as I struggled to pull my pants back on, sobbing, before crawling to a far corner.

The Ghaal exited my cage and made an obscene gesture with his hand and black tongue before the group left the way they had come, leaving me crying in a corner, the sound of my sobs echoing off the walls.

Ilk, where are you?

The next lot of footsteps came down the hall in a rush, and although it sounded like a single being, I couldn't bring myself to get out of the ball I had curled into in the corner of my cell.

"Human female," came a hiss, and I looked up to see Sol, his gray fingers wrapped around the bars of my cage. When I didn't answer, he repeated the sentiment.

"I have a name, not that you care," I mumbled. It seemed a petty thread to hold on to, but the pain and humiliation were still ripe within me.

"Human female, *please,* I'm risking my life being here. I'm trying to help you."

I managed to find the will to look up, and as I rolled out of my position, Sol was hovering his hand over the silver ball. There were no clicks, so the door was still locked. Was this a trap? I couldn't be sure, but I had to take the chance. Jumping to my feet, I ran to the bars, close to Sol but not so close he could reach me.

"Are you helping me? Why?"

His eyes as soulless as they appeared to me, looked pained. "I can't do this anymore. They intend to attempt to manually impregnate you rather than waiting until we are at the lab tomorrow. I told them it won't work, but they don't seem to care—"

My stomach dropped, and when I tried to speak, I made a choking noise. "They're going to..." I dry heaved at the reminder of their hands on me, "... rape me?"

"They suspect it might not work, but you're so very close to us physically, it is technically possible. They are doing it mainly for fun, I believe. They've waited a long time for your kind."

"Fun?" I cried out, grabbing the bars. *"Fun?"*

Sol hissed at me. *"Keep your voice down."*

"Why are you helping me?" I asked again. I wasn't satisfied with his answer, and although I was willing to take any help I could get, I couldn't be sure this wasn't a trap. The Ghaal had already tried lying to me to get me here, so how did I know this wasn't some sick game to them where they would hunt me down?

"Your Synth is near," Sol whispered, and my

heart skipped a beat. "But our camp is hidden. This may be your only chance. Once I open this cage, you are to run down the hallway you came from. You'll see doors at the end, but you mustn't stop. They are an illusion."

"An illusion? What?"

"Be quiet and listen to me! Yes, the doors are an illusion. We may have little technology left, but holograms we can do."

I had so many questions. "What's stopping the Synths from finding it?"

Sol looked impatient and rushed through his answer. "A combination of dumb luck and strategic plants they hate the scent of, which would cover your scent and ours. Now stop interrupting. You must run. Run until your legs burn. The second you feel the fresh air, call for your Synth. He will find you. He knows your scent, and once you break free of the shoghar bushes, he'll find you."

"They'll kill you," I mumbled. *Why did I care?* Perhaps because of the kindness this Ghaal was showing me. "I don't understand why you're helping me."

"I've seen many terrible things and taken part in more than I wish to admit." His eyes met mine as his fingers began to move over the silver ball. "I can't continue doing this. Maybe we aren't worth saving, after all."

"Are there others like you? Others who want to

help?" My fingers gripped the bars, and I ignored the burn, desperate to know. If there were a rebellion within the Ghaals, perhaps they would tear themselves apart from the inside.

"I have tried finding some, but it's dangerous. I risk exposing myself." He shook his head. "I don't think there are others who think like me. I'm sorry, I can see the hope in your eyes."

"Sol," I mumbled.

There was a series of clicks, and the cage door opened. "Go," Sol whispered, grabbing my shoulder and flinging me from the cage. "Go. *Now.*"

I wanted to tell him to come with me or say thank you or express my concern for his safety, but I wasn't the hero I had seen in movies and heard about in stories. I was frightened and weak on this planet, and I only hoped that the look we shared conveyed everything to Sol that I couldn't find the words to say.

His expression softened, and he nodded. "Go."

I ran.

CHAPTER 25

ILK

Vitri and I had followed the tracks from where Erica had been taken and were now pacing in large circles. The tracks were difficult to see even from the start and had faded in and out of obscurity over several yards until we couldn't find any further trace. There was no definite end to them, nowhere leading us to a trap door or a hideout but simply a footstep here and there, and then eventually, nothing.

"Did you know the Ghaal had a scout so close?" I asked Vitri, failing to keep the impatience from my tone.

His lifted his lip in distaste. "Not this close. They

haven't kept entirely to their colony and simply waited for the units to drop. As they became more desperate, they began spreading out... a race between us and them to find the units. But they know we're around, so they don't stay longer than they have to. I've never seen any evidence of a scout community here, no changes to the forest, and no drop in food or disturbances. As you said, they knew the females were coming, and they were the ones they'd been seeking. I can only assume they're making use of a previously abandoned building."

Even with the Moeks scrambling for time, bringing back species that were obviously of no help, biding their time in order to get more supplies, that couldn't have lasted forever.

Eventually, inevitably, more human females would have to be captured.

The Ghaal would have been ready for them.

But not ready for *us.*

They had the means to put us down, but as with all their technology, it was limited. I doubted their camps contained the weapons they needed to stop us. Vitri was right—they'd be occupying them only for as long as necessary.

"We should have taken weapons when we left," I mumbled, and Vitri shot me a surprised glance but said nothing. It was unlike us to seek violence, and after the forced actions of our escape from the colony, we swore it off. But the idea of Erica being taken from me had brought out the most possessive part of my nature, and I would do anything to get her back.

Even kill.

If she were harmed, there would be no reason for me not to kill them all.

If these scouting communities existed across the island, I was even more thankful my brothers and I were spread out. Their location choices would be limited, and as we continued to be watchful guardians over all kidnapped species, they would have to be cautious, limiting their activity.

But to take such a risk to obtain Erica? This only strengthened the knowledge that they were not only expecting the humans but knew exactly when they were coming. I still wondered why they brought only four instead of six, but that wasn't important right now.

Vitri cried out and clasped a hand over his nose. Instinctually, I took a whiff of the air and instantly regretted it, mimicking his action and trying not to dry heave. We had circled around again and walked straight through a section of forest populated with the shoghar bushes—large plants with deep green leaves and yellow veins that smelled like rotting flesh and bubbling acid. It was a scent I didn't need as it reminded me of the sections of the island that were uninhabitable long after the war, filled with the rotting corpses of those who died from disease.

The sickening scent made my stomach lurch, but I would search there as well and everywhere I could until I found Erica. Holding my breath for as long as I could, I circled the area, and finding nothing, I simply circled it again, my eyes watering and throat scratchy from the plants' scent.

I would keep searching until I couldn't walk, and then I would drag myself by my fingertips until they bled, and I still wouldn't stop until I found Erica. I recalled Erica's question about the technology the Ghaal possessed and why we hadn't taken any with us. I stood by my answer, but now I realized some sort of tracker would have been useful or some weapons. Even run-down technology was better than none, but we didn't want to turn into the very species we were trying to distance ourselves from.

I now realized passive, peaceful protest was no longer enough.

We doubled back over our tracks, ready to head back toward a small stream and then split up. Maybe after this was over, and Erica was back in my arms, a trip to the colony was called for to take what we needed.

Maybe it was time for a little war of our own.

"Ilk!"

Vitri and I looked up, and the thumping of my heart behind my ribs became too much to bear. Vitri's gaze settled on where the cry came from, and I almost dared to hope I hadn't imagined it.

"Was that..." he started.

"Ilk!"

"Erica!" I cried, bolting in the direction the cry came from.

She called again for me, and I responded as loud as I could. I heard a snap of relieved laughter followed by a sob, and when Erica burst through the low-hanging branches of a tree, I ran to her. Meeting her halfway when she weakened during her last few steps, her legs sagged once she saw me, and with an expression of determination, she leaped into my waiting arms. Her watery chuckles could barely be heard over the growling rumble that vibrated through my chest as I crushed her to me, ready to never let her go again.

"I'm sorry," she whispered against my shoulder as I ran my palm over her hair. "I'm so *so* sorry. I should never have walked away. Oh, Ilk."

I shushed her gently, turning to see Vitri watching me with a strange expression on his face. It looked almost like longing, and I wondered about my observation earlier concerning the one-sided affection between him and Tori. Once Erica's sobs had calmed slightly, I lowered her to the ground, but she grabbed at my arms and gripped onto my hand and forearm even as I straightened. Erica was desperate for comfort and security, and she could touch me anywhere she needed to.

Vitri approached Erica, and she looked at me for

reassurance before glancing back at him. "Hi," she whispered, hiccupping slightly. "I'm Erica."

"Erica," Vitri purred her name out, and I let a low snarl escape toward him. Erica was my female, my human, and she was not for him. He glanced at me, his lips curling into a smirk before he leaned back and took a step away from Erica. "I'm Vitri."

Erica wiped her face. "Did you find one of my friends?" she asked.

My heart swelled—her immediate thought was of her friends.

Vitri smirked again. "I found Tori."

Erica released a little *oh* sound, clapping her hand to her mouth. "Is she okay?"

"She's well. We'll go to her now."

Erica turned back to me and pulled on my arm until I bent down to her level. "Ilk, the Ghaal took me and—" She squealed as I gripped her hand too tight, and hastily I apologized, unable to stop the growl rumbling through my throat. "They were going to... they were going to..." She made a choking noise and shook her head. I didn't need her to say it, but instantly my blood boiled, and I tried to contain the feeling inside me.

"We don't need to talk about this now," I reassured her.

But she kept shaking her head, desperate to continue. "One of them, one of the Ghaal, he let me go."

Vitri's eyebrows shot up. "He *what?*"

She shook her head again, looking at the ground as if she couldn't understand it either. "He let me go. He said he couldn't stand to be part of it anymore. He risked his life." She glanced back the way she had come. "They probably killed him, Ilk," she said, desperation in her voice, still gripping my forearm. "Can we get out of here, please? What if they come after us?"

I snarled. They would know she would run straight to one of us, and they wouldn't come after her. Not right away. Tugging on Erica slightly so she followed, Vitri led us back to his home.

Vitri and I exchanged a look full of meaning.

A Ghaal with a conscience? If he tired of the experimentation, perhaps there were more who did too. Conflict within the colony could be useful.

As we walked, the thoughts cemented themselves in my mind.

I think the time had come for us to put this all to an end.

But first, all the females needed to be safe, and Erica and I would need to travel together.

I couldn't risk her being taken again.

"Tori!" Erica cried out as she ran toward the female, who was waiting at the base of a large tree, one foot resting on the tall roots and one hand clutching a spear. Tori dropped the weapon and ran toward her friend, pulling her into a hug.

"Oh my God, girl, it is *so* good to hear your voice," she said as Erica chuckled, tears running down her cheeks again. "I mean, literally. I only heard you speak once, and I had forgotten what you sounded like." Erica laughed again, and I relished the sound. When the women pulled out of the hug, they kept their hands on each other's arms for a moment before squeezing hands. They were holding onto the safety blanket that was their own kind. The reality that Erica may want to stay close to her friend hit me hard, and I barely contained my grimace as grief hit me in the chest.

"Samara? Misha?" Tori questioned.

Erica shook her head. "I was going to ask you the same thing. Ilk and I came here first to find the pod that was nearest to us, aside from the one on the other side of the mountains." She glanced at me, her expression halfway between hope and weariness. "Ilk says he has a brother on the other side of the mountain who would have gotten to that pod."

Tori threw a look at Vitri, who responded only with a smirk. "Lucky her." Her tone was deadpan.

"The other pod landed near the ocean on the other side of the Ghaal colony, we think."

"Those fucking creeps," Tori spat out. "Are you okay?" Again, she ran her hands up Erica's arms, and even the contact between the two women flared a possessiveness in me I had to fight to keep at bay.

"I'm okay, but I really think we need to find the others."

"Agreed."

They turned to face us, and I chuckled at the difference in their stance. Tori had her arms crossed over her chest, one hip pivoted higher than the other. The pose screamed attitude, but when I glanced at Vitri, he seemed to take this only as a challenge. His grin didn't waver, and after they stared at each other for a beat, I could have sworn I saw a shadow of a smile cross Tori's face. Perhaps she was warming up to him more than she wanted to admit.

On the other hand, Erica gazed at me with affection and a hint of sorrow that made my heart ache.

"We'll make a plan," I said, approaching Erica and grabbing her upper arm gently, steering her away from the others. "But I need to talk to you first."

"Oh, okay." She sounded uncertain, and I said nothing as I led her some paces away until we could no longer hear the chatter of Vitri.

Turning, I sat on a large root, and pulled Erica

toward me when she hovered hesitantly, barely within my reach. She stepped closer until her legs were between mine and our faces level. Mimicking Tori's motions, I ran my hands up and down Erica's arms, a rumble starting in my chest at how she shuddered under my touch, a flare of her arousal hitting the air.

"Are you okay?" I muttered, checking her for any sign of injury.

"A little shaken, but I'm fine." Her voice was barely a whisper, and she grabbed my face and forced me to look at her, her small hands barely encompassing my cheeks. "Ilk, I'm sorry I ran from you. I was upset. I should have stayed and talked it out."

I shook my head. "No, Erica, I should apologize. I should've explained everything to you from the start, including my species and all the things you needed to know about us. I was selfish. I wanted to keep you with me as long as I could, and I'm sorry."

She frowned. "Keep me with you?"

"Not prisoner," I said, my eyes roaming her body. I added with a smirk, "Although the thought did cross my mind." She chuckled quietly, and I was pleased. "I wanted you to stay with me, but I'll understand if you want to stay with Tori." Even as I said it, I hated the words. Erica was safer with me, and maybe now she would understand the danger she was in from the Ghaal. We needed to spread out, to stay apart, much as my brothers and I had done for years but not forever. We could make a long-term plan later, but for now, it was better if we separated and kept moving. I sighed, at the very least. Erica needed to have a choice. "Tori is your kind after all, and I'm..."

"My big rock alien?" It was my turn to frown, and she laughed quietly, smoothing her thumbs over my brow. "Ilk..." she took a deep breath, "... I *do* want to stay with you, but I also want to be with the girls as well, so maybe we can work something out."

We could work something out because I would do anything, change anything if it meant I got to keep Erica by my side. Without another word, I wrapped my arms around her and pulled her against my body. She collided with me and huffed out a laugh as I squeezed her, and she ran her small hands around my back, teasing my skin.

"My pheromones are stronger because of how I feel about you," I muttered against her hair.

There was a sharp intake of breath from her, and her hands stilled their ministrations. "And how do you feel about me?"

With a deep growl, I ran my hands down her back and over her soft ass, pulling her against me harder. "Let me show you."

"No," she whispered.

"No?" When I pulled back, she was smiling.

I didn't understand.

Had I upset her?

"Let me show *you.*"

She sunk to her knees in front of me, placed her hands on my thighs, and spread my legs. A deep frown was still on my face as I watched her motions, and when she pulled my loincloth to the side and traced her fingers up my length, I snarled and snatched her hand. "You don't have to do anything you don't want to, Errrica."

"I want to. I want to show you how *I* feel."

I loosened my grip on her, and slowly she pulled her hand from mine, running her fingers along the inside of my palm as she did. Her smile was coy, and when she wrapped both hands around my cock, my hips bucked up into her grip. Her touch was so achingly gentle. I gripped the root I sat on, the wood crunching under my hands into splintered shards as she ran her tongue around the head of my cock.

"Errrica," I panted out, the rumble of a growl working through my chest as she awoke me—mind, body, and soul. "I need to fuck you."

"Soon, big boy, just let me take care of you first." Her breath was hot against my skin, and I thrust my hips toward her mouth again, unable to contain myself. I had been faced with the prospect of losing her forever, and it had only cemented my desire to keep her close.

Then she had said it, *I do want to stay with you,* and everything I had been trying to keep below the surface while Vitri and I searched for her came tumbling forth. When Erica placed her lips around my cock, pulling the head into her mouth, I lost what little self-control I had left.

I placed a hand on the back of her head and thrust forward, causing her to squeak in alarm before the sound faded into a satisfied hum as her mouth bobbed up and down on my shaft. Her mouth was hot and wet around me, and she held my eye contact as the head of my cock disappeared beyond those gorgeous pink lips over and over again.

I couldn't take it anymore.

Wrapping a hand around her neck, I lifted Erica from her knees, standing until her toes were dragging on the ground. Her fingers squeezed around my wrist, and I huffed out ragged breaths, the scent of her arousal had driven me beyond the edge. Keeping one hand around her throat, I used the other to undo her pants and shove them down just enough to expose her to me. I would take my time with her later and show her a thousand times with my tongue how much I wanted her to stay with me.

But this time, I needed to claim her.

With a hard shove, she fell back to her knees, and I fell to mine, grabbing her hips and turning her around. I placed a palm between her shoulder blades and pushed until she bent over, and I was met with a flush of her scent as her arousal peaked. Running a finger between the lips of her cunt, she groaned when I dipped the tip of my finger inside before removing it and sucking off the delicious flavor of her.

She was ready for me.

With as much control as I could manage, I placed the head of my cock at the entrance of her tight cunt and held her hips as I pushed forward. Her small hands scrambled against the forest floor, grabbing and releasing handfuls of leaves and small plants, soil embedding itself under her nails as she cried out.

Seated fully inside her, I wasted no time and pulled out again before pushing back in harder than before. She squealed and moaned. I angled her hips to allow myself the best access to her and began pounding into her slick wetness, feeling her opening up to the thick intrusion.

"Fuck, *yes,* Ilk." She hissed through her teeth as I increased my speed.

Bending over her, encompassing her body with mine, I planted my fists on the ground on either side of her hands, continuing to thrust into her and groaning at the way she arched her back. We were both no more than animals as I claimed her as mine.

Mine.

CHAPTER 26

ERICA

Ilk shifted his angle behind me and roughly shoved my legs apart to allow access for his hand. Expertly, he found my clit and assaulted it with his fingers, rubbing in small, tight circles and not letting up the speed with which he fucked me. The ground was digging into my knees through my pants, pulled halfway down in his haste, but I didn't care.

If I thought Ilk fucked me hard last time—it was nothing compared to now.

He had lost control, and the sounds he made were so *animalistic* it turned me on more than I would like to admit. The combination of his cock stretching me open, hitting every sensitive spot inside, and his fingers on my clit was too much. I shuddered and cried out, eventually biting into my wrist to cover the moans as I trembled and came around him.

He responded with a deep resonating growl and leaned forward again, shifted the angle, wrapped his arms around my body, held on, and plowed into me. I was a mess, uttering a sequence of nonsensical obscenities and praises as my high was drawn out. With a roar he didn't bother to cover, I heard the sounds of several small animals fleeing the area as he came, the clear cum spilling out of my pussy when he pulled out, making a mess of my legs and the forest floor.

I squeaked as Ilk wrapped an arm around my waist and pulled me on top of him as he collapsed onto the ground, turning me so we were chest to chest. I wrapped my arms around his body as best I could and sighed in contentment, pressing my ear against his hard muscles to listen to the dull thud of his heart as it slowed down with his breathing.

"Did I hurt you?" His voice rumbled as he spoke, the syllables still heavy with a growled edge to them that made my heart flutter with desire.

"No," I said, squirming against him. "You're amazing."

He hummed in response, pulling me tighter against him. "I want to fuck you every chance I get for as long as you'll have me." I planted a kiss on his chest and returned my cheek to the spot so I could listen to his body when another hum rumbled through him. "I'm sorry," he muttered after a moment of silence.

"For what?" I lifted my head and rested my chin on my hand, looking up at his face.

"For not wanting to let you go. You only trusted me because you had no choice. I need you to know if you want to leave, I won't stop you, but I won't lie and tell you I wouldn't miss you. It's dangerous out there, but I'll admit my desire to keep you close is selfish."

I lifted myself so I could kiss his cool lips, and he opened his eyes to meet mine, the bright green blazing. He was right. I trusted him out of necessity because I was thrown into a situation where I was utterly helpless, and he was the only one not trying to hurt me. But somewhere along the way, I'd cemented a bond with this alien in a few days stronger than anything I'd ever had with any other partner. We had all the time in the world to figure out what this was, and I was here for it.

"I'm not going anywhere," I said, giggling as he closed his eyes again, that big goofy grin lighting his face. "But..." I sat up, straddling him. "We really should get back to the others. We need a plan to find the last two girls."

When he sat, I didn't move, so we wound up chest to chest again, my breasts pushed against the hard, flat plane of his chest. He still smelled amazing. I flicked his braid over his shoulder, buried my face in the crook of his neck, inhaled deeply, and let the scent linger over me, sending a tingle down my spine and between my legs. His hands tightened around my thighs, and he growled. "Careful, Errrica," he grumbled, his fingers flexed on my legs. "I can smell your arousal, and I might have to take you again."

I responded by grinding my hips against his lap, and Ilk snarled at the sensation, his still exposed cock rubbing between my legs. "Errrrrrica," he protested, his fingers twitching on my legs and the growl in his voice drawing out the 'r' in my name further.

"I'm sorry," I whispered against his neck. "I couldn't help it."

Despite the dull ache between my legs, I wanted to take him again. He was right—the pheromones only increased what I already felt, and as my feelings for Ilk had intensified, so had my need for him. Being this close with the warmth of his body encompassing mine, I couldn't get enough. I yelped when he stood, and I slid from his lap. Ilk smirked and held a hand out to me, helping me to my feet. The second I stood, he pulled me against him, and his erection rubbed against my stomach.

"There'll be plenty of time for me to fuck you until you can't move, Errrica. Plenty of time." He growled next to my ear, finishing with a huff of warm breath that left my legs weak. When he pulled away, I barely contained my whimper, biting my lip before frowning as he chuckled at me.

With a snarl of my own, I reached out and grabbed his cock through his loincloth. "You know, two can play at that game, Ilk. I can tease you as much as you tease me."

His laugh was dark as he grabbed, lifted, and slammed my back against a tree and moved until I was crushed between his body and the trunk with his cock pressed between my legs so he could grind against me. "Yes." He growled with a thrust against my body that knocked the air from my lungs. "But only one of us can pin the other one down and fuck them senseless."

I grinned.

Okay, so he had me there.

Sitting next to Tori, she threw me a sideways glance but otherwise said nothing about my little excursion with Ilk. I wondered if she had slept with Vitri and, if not, was she tempted to. Smirking to myself, I huffed out a breath of amusement when I realized I was simply looking for reassurance that I wasn't the only one who came undone so easily under the flirtatious alien who had rescued me. I watched Vitri, and he was eyeing Tori as she rewound the rope around the top of her new spear.

Vitri wasn't unattractive. Like Ilk, he was tall and larger than life with a barrel-like chest and arms that would be intimidating as hell if I didn't know the being behind them was so gentle. But that and the green eyes were where the similarities ended. Rather than the harsh, sharp edges of his face, like stone that was Ilk, Vitri had a more boyish face, mischief in his eyes as he smirked more often than he had a neutral expression. His skin was patterned with what I had originally thought were tattoos until I later realized they were actual vines that appeared to grow out of him and melded in with his skin when he wasn't using them, I guessed. Every now and then, a small pink flower would unfurl from one of the vines, and sometimes he would pick it off and discard it with little interest. His skin was an earthy green, and where Ilk had a single braid, Vitri had many intertwined with the vines that were a part of him.

Damn, Ilk wasn't kidding when he said they changed to their environment.

Tori dropped her spear. "So, what's the plan?"

"We split up," I said immediately, earning myself another eyebrow raise from Tori. "Ilk and I will go to the other side of the mountains because Ilk knows that territory to find whoever landed there. You and Vitri head toward the ocean to scour that area."

Vitri nodded and hadn't taken his eyes off Tori.

"We need to keep moving." I turned to Ilk as his deep voice rumbled between us. He held my eye contact, his gaze sad and apologetic. "We'll go find your friends, but we can't stay together. We need to keep the Ghaal off our trail."

I frowned. "So we just keep walking around and camping out forever?"

"Not forever. Just for a few days or weeks. The Ghaal won't give up on finding you, but we can't make it easy for them. Then we'll come back together and figure out a way to keep you all safe, indefinitely."

Ilk and Vitri exchanged a look full of meaning, and my brows furrowed together, wanting to know what they were thinking. I was about to ask when Tori cleared her throat.

"I think I can go by myself. Vitri should stay here and watch the forest now we know the Ghaal have a camp so close."

"No." Tori glanced up at my command, surprised and slightly insulted. "No," I repeated, placing a hand on her arm. "This is an alien planet, Tori, and we shouldn't be going anywhere alone. Vitri can protect you."

"I can protect myself."

"While you're right..." Vitri chimed in, his eyes serious but his smirk betraying him, "... and I've seen you in action, I do agree with Erica. I'm not leaving you to wander alone, especially closer to the Ghaal colony."

"Fine." Tori huffed out a breath, but before she looked back at her hands in her lap, she shared a glance with Vitri, and I narrowed my eyes, hiding my smirk. I didn't know Tori all that well, but I think I knew her well enough to know she'd kick my ass if I pointed out she was blushing at the idea of spending more alone time with Vitri. The spark of interest in her eyes made me shut my mouth when I almost suggested she come with Ilk and me.

"When do we leave?" I asked, directing my question at Ilk.

"Tomorrow. You need to rest."

"Honestly, I just want to get out of here."

Ilk watched me with sympathy shining through his bright green eyes but shook his head and simply repeated. "You need to rest."

Again, I huffed out a breath, releasing a small "harrumph" sound, but I knew he was right. Once I had sat next to Tori, the fatigue had caught up with me, coming down from the adrenaline of escape. But I didn't feel safe here. I felt the Ghaal were watching us from behind every tree and out of every shadow. I didn't like the forest, and while I knew they wouldn't attack with Ilk right next to me, the sense of my skin crawling wouldn't go away until we left this place far behind us.

the sense of my skin crawling wouldn't go away until we left this place far behind us.

CHAPTER 27

ILK

Tori and Vitri split off from Erica and me early in our journey when we were just past the boundaries of the forest. They would need to skirt around the fields and the woodlands in order to get to the ocean. There were few points of access that weren't riddled with cliff faces, and since they also needed to avoid the Ghaal colony, their journey would take them an additional day or two, depending on how fast they moved. Tori seemed capable enough, and I had noticed that she scowled at Vitri as often as she offered him a genuine smile. I preferred my Erica, softer and gentler but playful with me.

Neither of the women was overly pleased with

the idea that we wouldn't be getting together and forming a colony of our own, not yet, at least. Vitri and I agreed we were to make sure the other human females were safe, but after that, we needed to split up again once we had discussed our plans.

I liked the idea of being alone with Erica and squeezed her hand as we walked. She looked up and offered me one of her smiles, and I returned the look. She already appeared tired, but I knew she would push herself to get back to our cave as fast as she could manage. I would then insist she rest for a day before we began to make our way around the mountain. I would offer her to bathe in the spring with me, and a rumble ran through my chest at the idea of getting her naked again. Erica looked up at me and smirked as if she knew exactly what I was thinking.

Before we had split ways, I had discussed with Vitri my thoughts on invading the colony for weapons. He looked uncertain, but after one glance at the females, he nodded. We would discuss it at length later once we each located the two remaining women and were certain the Ghaal weren't tracking us. I didn't think they had the technology remaining to track, but then again, I also didn't think they had cloaking technology, and I had been proven wrong in the worst possible way.

As the sun neared the top of its arc across the sky, Erica squeezed my hand and tugged on my arm, pulling me to stop. "Look." She pointed with her spear. "Gorae."

I had noticed the herd as we approached but hadn't planned on hunting just yet. "Are you hungry?"

In response, her stomach rumbled, and it had been difficult for me not to constantly remind her that plants alone were not enough to survive on here. She shuffled her feet, glancing between her spear and the small fluffy creatures. "I am, but I don't know if I'm ready to kill yet. I might cry."

Pursing my lips, I watched Erica closely. I didn't want her to be upset, but the reality was she would need to learn to fend for herself. I had no plans of going anywhere, but as fragile and helpless as she was, I wanted to teach her as many skills as possible. While my planet was a mix of species from across the galaxies, none of them were as out of place and weak as Erica and her companions. Their skin was not made to survive the outdoors without additional protection, she could not adapt, and she had no defense mechanisms. I ached for her because the determination was in her face to do better, to make this work, and while I was elated that she chose to be here with *me,* she didn't belong.

I shouldn't push her.

But I would look after her, always and forever.

"Errrica..." I grumbled when the emotion bubbled in my chest, watching her stare at her spear, intentionally crafted smaller for her frame.

She smirked at me. "Don't you use your *fuck me* voice right now." She pressed against me, leaning her arm into mine with our fingers still intertwined. The contact sent tingles through my skin, and my chest rumbled with a growl that made her laugh.

Erica, my mate, I will *protect her.*

"I will get you some food, Erica." I put a hand on her shoulder and pushed gently so she sat where she was on a small ridge, could overlook the herd, and wouldn't lose sight of me, nor I her. Slowly, I descended the small hill, spear at the ready, and approached the herd. Farther out than I would have liked, they became aware of my approach and began to scatter. Launching my spear, I caught one in its hindquarters, and I flinched at the bleating cry of pain it released. I quickly made my way over to the gorae, removed the spear, and finished the kill as quickly as possible. I never wanted to cause unnecessary pain, and perhaps after all, I understood some humans' desires to not eat meat.

When I turned, Erica was gone, and with a roar, I slung my kill over my shoulder and bolted back toward where I left her. As I approached, my heart ready to burst from my chest at the idea of losing her again, Erica reappeared over the small ridge, her arms laden with broken branches. She stopped in her tracks at the look on my face.

"I'm sorry," she said, dropping the wood. "I

thought you might need to make a fire, and I wanted to help. Ilk…" Erica kicked her boot against the grass before looking back at me, the sorrow in her eyes enough to quench the reprimand at the edge of my tongue for her leaving my sight. "If I'm going to stay with you, I don't want to be a burden. I don't expect you to do everything. I just ask for your patience as this is all new to me."

Dropping the gorae to the dirt with a thud, I closed the gap between us with two large steps and wrapped my arms around Erica, crushing her against my body. She tilted her beautiful face up to me, her confused smile evaporating as I leaned in and swiped my tongue across her lips, enticing her to open them. She did, and I plunged my tongue into her mouth, drinking in all the sounds of pleasure she made.

When we broke apart, she asked, "What was that for?"

"I will look after you, Erica. Always."

She nodded, leaned her cheek against my chest, and huffed out a satisfied hum. A pleasured growl moved through my chest. She wanted to help. She knew I would do anything for her, and Erica still wanted to help.

We would make a good team, her and me.

Erica, my mate.

CHAPTER 28

ERICA

We made good time returning to the mountains.

Only camping one night on the way back, we arrived home before the sun had finished setting. I never thought I would be so damn happy to see a freaking *cave*, but it screamed *safe* and *home* to me now, and I just wanted to stay and bask in the hot springs and the sunshine.

But there would be time for that later because we needed to find whoever landed on the other side of the mountains. Then apparently, we'd be going on an extended camping trip. Part of me was excited to see more of this planet, but there was the fear plucking at my chest, reminding me of the dangers of this place.

Then I'd look at Ilk and remember his promise to protect me.

There was also more than a big part of me that simply wanted to stay here. There was no wondering what the next day brought, how I was going to pay an unexpected bill, or what movie was on. I would be lying if I said there weren't many things I would miss about Earth, but there was a freedom here. On top of that, I was protected and safe with Ilk, and I'd never felt such comfort before.

And there were ways of keeping ourselves entertained.

Lifting my water bag, I finished the last few gulps and smacked my lips loudly, drawing an amused smirk from Ilk. "So…" I said, flinging the strap over my shoulder again, "… do we grab some supplies and get going?" I was sure if I stopped for too long, I wouldn't want to get up and leave again. The guilt in my gut flared once more. I was safe and comfortable, but what of Misha and Samara? Ilk had assured me his brother on the other side of the mountains would have whoever landed there, and they'd be safe, and Tori and Vitri were on their way to the coast to search for the occupant of the fourth pod.

Maybe I could rest a few days like some sort of fucked-up honeymoon.

No.

"I think a quick rest will be enough. I really don't want to..." My words drained away at the look on Ilk's face. His anger melted into shock at my keenness to keep moving, and I raised my eyebrows at him.

"You need to rest," he stated.

"You keep saying that." I was seconds away from stomping my foot on the ground in frustration. I was conflicted, but I needed to do the right thing. There was no question really, even though I had suffered a moment of weakness, I would find my friends and make sure they were safe. "But somewhere around this mountain is a friend of mine, and I've already waited too long."

Without a word, Ilk swept me up with one arm and flung me over his shoulder. I struggled and hit his back as he began walking through the rocky ridges, although I had no real intention of trying to hurt him, more to physically indicate my frustration because, at this point, I didn't know how else to release it. The slap-in-the-face realization after the past few days that I wasn't as physically fit as I thought I was had been an unwelcome reality check, and I felt like I was holding Ilk back. Who knows, without me, he could've walked across this entire place and rescued everyone in the time it took us to get to Tori. Not only that, I was worried. What if the other girls hadn't found Synths to look after them? While Tori and I had been lucky, they may not have been. What if the Ghaal had got to them first?

Guilt hung heavy in my stomach. I couldn't shift it, and every passing minute made it worse. I wanted to stay here with Ilk, but what kind of person would that make me? I couldn't live with myself if I did that. I should have been searching for the other girls from the start and insisted we go straightaway. We should have gone around the mountains first because Tori was fine.

The fact I knew I had no way of knowing that at the time didn't soothe my guilt.

Ilk ignored my attempts to fight him off when he lifted me off his shoulder and pulled my cloak over my head. I beat my fists weakly against his shoulders as he bent to remove my boots and pants, and with a flick, he stood and undid the strip of fabric around my chest. "*Ilk*, talk to me." Tears were building up behind my eyes, and I hated it as if I didn't feel weak enough without crying again.

"You will be no good to anyone if you are exhausted. We stay here tonight and go tomorrow." His lip lifted into a scowl. "Although I would rather you rest for a few days, I will accept one night of rest."

Glaring at him, it was hard to argue. He had unknowingly reflected my desire to stay here for a few days at least, but my desires were selfish and made me think I was an awful person. If that's how

I felt just *thinking* about doing it, I can't imagine how I could bear to actually stay here when they needed help. I still struggled with Ilk when he grabbed me by my waist, lifted me again as if I weighed nothing, and took me around the corner before unceremoniously dropping me into a hot spring.

Bursting to the surface, I spluttered and splashed about, trying to get my footing, and frowned at the smirk on Ilk's face as he removed his boots and loincloth.

"Was that really necessary?" I spluttered at him, moving away as he lowered himself into the spring next to me.

He simply kept smirking, and I found it hard to keep the smile from my face at his cheekiness. Without even trying, he had disarmed me, stopped all the conflict, guilt, and dread building up in me, knowing I needed rest and to be cared for.

The trick now would be to *allow* myself to be cared for.

It was one night.

Ilk was insisting I rest for *one night*, and he was right—I would be no good to the other girls if I passed out from exhaustion.

Ilk reached into a pouch hanging from his loincloth on the side of the spring and withdrew a handful of root berries before pressing his hands together and releasing the oils. He reached toward me, and I crossed my arms over my chest and pouted at him. He laughed. "Are you going to let me wash you, or am I going to have to tie you down?"

A shudder ran down my spine until my pussy tingled at his words. Dammit, that should not turn me on. "Fine," I said, dropping my hands to my sides as Ilk approached, placing his hands on my shoulders and rubbing the oil down my arms. He let me take over as he undid my braids, pulling out leaves and twigs as he came across them.

"I will redo your hair tonight. Usually, the braids would last longer than this, but..."

"Usually, one isn't taken hostage by Ghaal. I know." I grunted as Ilk grabbed me, pulling me against his chest. With a soft chuckle, I placed my hands on his chest and pushed away just enough to look up at him. "It's okay, Ilk. I'm okay."

"I can't risk losing you again. Maybe I should search for the other human alone."

Shoving him harder this time, I stepped away and glided through the warm water. "Are you serious? No. I have to come with you. I need to know they're okay. Now more than ever."

"Erica—"

"No," I said the word again, this time holding up a finger between us, ignoring the flash of anger on Ilk's face. The moment was strange to me because Ilk could easily crush me, take me hostage, or even kill me if he wished. But I was scolding him, absolutely no fear within me. I was safe with Ilk and always would be. "No. This isn't up for discussion. Don't you think I'm safer with you, anyway? Rather than wandering around here gathering food and water, waiting for you to return?"

"I will stock the cave with food. You won't have to leave."

"I am *not* being locked up in a cave. Besides, I have to be there since they don't know you. You might frighten them." He threw me a look that hinted he was about to argue. "No more talk about this. *End of discussion.*"

The water slapped against my chest as he rushed forward and pushed me against the side of the spring. Ilk stared down at me with such intensity I almost shrunk under his gaze, and with a grunt, he reached forward and finished undoing my braids.

"I'll protect you," he grumbled, barely more than a mumble.

"What was that?"

"*I* will *protect you.*" He was like an errant child throwing a tantrum, not getting his way, and trying his best to pretend he was okay with it.

"Damn straight you will. You'll protect me while we look for the next girl *together.*"

He simply huffed out a snort, grumbled something I couldn't hear, and continued combing through my hair. Slowly, the silence that fell between us ebbed from frustrated to comfortable, and I relaxed against the side of the spring as Ilk finished combing the braids from my hair. When I tried to grab some root berries to wash it, he shoved my hands away with another grumble and did it for me. *Fine, I'll let him wash me if it's what he needed to satiate whatever possessive urges were running through his mind.*

Ilk finished washing me, and apparently, it wasn't enough to satiate him.

I gripped his shoulders as his hand moved under the water, swirling gentle circles against my stomach before drifting between my legs. I moaned, and he rumbled out a growl.

"I'll protect you, Errrica," he mumbled again, brushing his finger against my clit and eliciting a gasp from me.

"I know you will, Ilk," I whispered, barely able to catch my breath as he carefully pushed a finger inside me. "Oh *fuck.*"

As he started pumping his finger, then lifted me to my toes and wrapped his other arm around me, stilling my movements as I tried to squirm against him. He thumbed my clit, and captured my mouth in his when I moaned loudly.

"I'll take care of you, Errrrrrica." There was more intensity in his growls now, and it matched the pace he was fucking his finger into me, his breath hot against my ear.

"I know, I know. Just... oh please..."

He hummed, and my fingers gripped against his skin, relishing in the stone-like texture that was comforting to me now.

I was safe.

With Ilk, I was forever safe.

Safe and... *oh God...*

"Come for me, my mate," he demanded.

And I did.

EPILOGUE

ERICA

Stretching, I awoke as the first sun was barely peeking over the horizon, the orange glow casting long shadows across the base of the mountains and scarcely offering a misty light around the cave. Ilk was already awake and leaned over to gently kiss my lips before I got dressed. I had slept well, amazingly well. Cuddled up against the warmth of Ilk, tired on the back of a handful of orgasms, and the winds outside drowned out by the boulder blocking the entrance.

Every time we had sex, he was less gentle, less cautious that he was going to break me, and it was better each time, even when I thought it couldn't possibly be.

Before we retired to bed last night, Ilk and I moved across the flat plains of the foothills to collect some food. Unlike the journey to the forest, while food would still be available as we traveled around the mountain, it wouldn't be quite as abundant, and having supplies would mean less time wasted if we couldn't immediately come across what we needed.

Besides, I wanted to be able to have something to offer whichever girl we came across—Samara or Misha—just in case they hadn't had access to food and water like I did.

Ilk looked unhappy at the amount I chose to carry, but I refused to let him be burdened with everything we needed, although he made it clear the weight was nothing to him. I wanted to at least try, and if it got too much, then I would relent and offload some of my supplies to him.

I still carried my spear, even though I hadn't found the courage to use it yet.

My hair was freshly braided, and for the dozenth time since waking, I ran my hand appreciatively over the braids, always impressed that Ilk could achieve such an intricate style with his large fingers.

"Ready?" Ilk asked, and as I nodded, he rolled the boulder in front of the door to his cave. He snatched up my hand, held onto it tightly, and we began walking over the rocky ridges toward the Ghaal colony. Although we would turn away long before we reached it, the knowledge we were heading toward them still made my skin crawl. The orange intensity of their eyes was burned into my mind, and the way the one who looked at me when he came into my cage with all sorts of horrible intentions planned for later that night...

Thank God for Sol.

I wondered what happened to him and if he had escaped with his life. Somehow, I doubted it. He had let me go, and I'm sure that was nothing short of treason. But part of me liked to think he had somehow got away and was living on the beach somewhere. Wishful thinking, but it eased my guilt slightly at being the reason for his death.

Ilk and I walked for over an hour, and I became tired faster than I had when heading to the forest. The side of the mountain was not a smooth journey through a field, and we'd probably only traveled half the distance we would have if we were on a flat plain as we were constantly stepping around—or in Ilk's case, sometimes *over*—rocks and small boulders. Eventually, I needed to let go of Ilk's hand as I needed both of mine to balance when I followed him through the terrain. As things became harder, Ilk walked behind me, ready to catch me if I slipped.

Ilk believed we should reach Lanir's territory before nightfall, and I was thankful this wasn't another two-day journey. At that point, we would set up for the night and then begin to scour the local area in the morning.

The sun was beginning its slow descent in the late afternoon when a creature burst out from a cave I didn't even notice, more of a crevice between two boulders, snarling and grabbing me before I was lifted from my feet. As I screamed, Ilk roared and snatched at the arms of the creature. They were similar in size, but this being had no hair, and while his eyes were the same bright green as Ilk's, his skin was darker, a layered, textured gray that appeared ashy. He had bright orange lines running across his body like etched tattoos, and when he looked at me, he was positively fearsome, and I screamed again.

Ilk shouted something at the creature in his language, and it looked at him, then back at me still held in his hands. Ilk was poised with his spear at the creature's back but hesitant to attack. We were near an edge, and if I was dropped suddenly, I might not be able to regain my footing in time.

"Ilk!" I cried as the creature's grip on me tightened. I grabbed his forearms, and he shot me a look so full of anger and emotion when I released a startled squeak. Ilk was cautious, but he wasn't moving, and I took a moment to take a deep breath and study the creature.

The bright green eyes, so much like Ilk's...

... in fact, *exactly* like Ilk's.

When I studied the coloring of his skin more closely, the orange wasn't like tattoos. In fact, it looked exactly like a rock that had cracked apart, exposing lines of lava underneath.

"Lanir?" I whispered, trying my best to get the pronunciation right.

His manic eyes settled on mine, and while his breathing was still heavy, his grip eased slightly. "She said there were others. I didn't realize you would come so soon. We are leaving the mountains again. The Ghaal know we're here."

Ilk stepped forward as Lanir returned me to my feet, my head spinning as I tried to take in his words and moved around him to be by Ilk's side. I trusted Lanir because Ilk did, but it didn't make his appearance or aggressive mannerisms any less intimidating. "The Ghaal?" Ilk grumbled out.

Lanir nodded, and they shared a significant look.

"Who's with you?" I asked. Whatever Ilk and Lanir needed to discuss, they could do it later. Lanir said *we* and, therefore, he must have found someone.

"I'm here," a small voice spoke up.

And I turned toward the voice.

I didn't know much about her, only assumptions I could make based on our limited communication while we were captive on the Moeks' ship. The woman staring at me now, a knowing smile lifting the corner of her lips, is far from what I expected to see when we found her.

Quiet Samara, naïve Samara, was draped in furs of her own and carried a knife that appeared too large for her. She looked every bit the warrior princess I'd imagined myself to be a few days ago. Hardened by her environment but throwing a look of such affection at Lanir, it threw me off guard. He looked like a demon from a fantasy novel, but the way Samara gazed at him, he could've been Prince Charming. Gray lines streaked Samara's face, but not as though she was dirty—it looked more like war paint.

I smiled back at her, and Samara held her arms out for a hug as she moved toward me.

THE END

Continue with...
Rescuer – Elements of Abduction Book 2
for
Tori and Vitri's story

This enemies to lovers alien abduction novel will have you wondering what other creative ways Vitri can use his vines.

ACKNOWLEDGMENTS

✦

Thank you for reading. I hope you enjoyed the first in this series of spicy alien standalones.

I've been wanting to release a steamy alien romance for a while now, waiting to come up with the perfect starter. When the idea of aliens who adapted to their environment sprung to the forefront of my mind, it was on. I don't think I've ever written a first draft as quickly as I did. I was so excited to get this story out.

And beyond that, it's opened up an entire galaxy—pun intended—of possibilities. I *love* paranormal romance, and I'm excited to be expanding my universe to SciFi romance. I'll still keep writing demons and angels, but now there are aliens too, and there'll be more creatures to come.

Stefanie Dawn

Because we don't discriminate here.
Monster lovers unite!

CONNECT WITH ME ONLINE

ANGELS AND FIRE BOOKS

Find our exciting stories at:

www.angelsandfirebooks.com.au

READER GROUP

Want access to fun, prizes and sneak peeks?

Stefanie Dawn

Join my Facebook Reader Group.
https://www.facebook.com/groups/588038442170571

NEWSLETTER

Sign up for my Newsletter.
https://www.subscribepage.com/angelsandfirebooks

BOOKBUB

https://www.bookbub.com/authors/stefanie-dawn

GOODREADS

Add my books to your TBR list
on my Goodreads profile.
https://www.goodreads.com/author/
show/21761217.Stefanie_Dawn

AMAZON

https://www.amazon.com/author/stefaniedawn

WEBSITE

http://www.angelsandfirebooks.com.au/

INSTAGRAM

https://www.instagram.com/angelsandfirebooks

EMAIL

info@angelsandfirebooks.com.au

FACEBOOK

https://www.facebook.com/stefaniedawnwriter

ABOUT THE AUTHOR

Stefanie Dawn has been a writer and creative soul all her life **and** strives to give her readers stories they can escape into as they become absorbed in the worlds created.

When she isn't writing, Stefanie might be painting, reading, or watching movies. She loves the process of producing films as another form of storytelling. There's also a good chance she'll be baking some delicious treats—pretending she won't later regret consuming them—or simply enjoying a cocktail with friends.

Stefanie Dawn lives in South Australia with her ever-supportive partner and a lovable gang of rescue cats.

You can stay up to date with
Stefanie and her books at:
www.angelsandfirebooks.com.au